MORE
LIMEHOUSE NIGHTS

THOMAS BURKE

By Thomas Burke

LIMEHOUSE NIGHTS:
    TALES OF CHINATOWN

MORE LIMEHOUSE NIGHTS

TWINKLETOES

NIGHTS IN TOWN:
    A LONDON AUTOBIOGRAPHY

LONDON LAMPS:
    A BOOK OF SONGS

OUT AND ABOUT:
    MORE NIGHTS IN TOWN

THE SONG BOOK OF QUONG LEE OF
    LIMEHOUSE

THE OUTER CIRCLE:
    RAMBLES IN REMOTE LONDON

MORE
LIMEHOUSE NIGHTS

BY

THOMAS BURKE
AUTHOR OF "LIMEHOUSE NIGHTS," ETC.

NEW  YORK
GEORGE H. DORAN COMPANY

Published by
Wildside Press, LLC
P.O. Box 301
Holicong, PA 18928-0301 USA
www.wildsidepress.com

Wildside Press Edition: MMIII

TO
WINIFRED

CONTENTS

CONTENTS

THE YELLOW SCARF

THE YELLOW SCARF

THE shape and soul of Shadwell are reflected in its name. Shadwell! Cold, grey, stony syllables, without lustre or savour; flat to the eye and the palate. It lies derelict between the river and Commercial Road. Its main streets are forlorn and bleak of aspect, and are named in cruel mockery—Formosa Terrace, Acacia Grove, Plum-tree Walk, Laburnum Court. Its dominant odours are fried fish and bilge-water. Its colour by day is of cobweb; by night, of the jungle. Its noise is persistent; a brown drone overriden by intermittent crashes. It is sliced at intervals by alleys without light, whose silence is not peace, but silence so tense that one knows it must soon be broken by some sound of dread. On the flood-tide floats from Limehouse the bitter-sweet alluring smell of Asia; and the spring comes slowly up this way.

It is a circus of harsh, unavailing endeavour. Here wealth does not accumulate, though men decay. Its people are casual labourers, outcasts, petty thieves, ineffectual shopkeepers. They are for ever splashily busy, without aim or hope, in this and that puny enterprise; and are perpetually harassed in chasing the cocky and elusive one-and-sixpence. Their evenings are as stressful as their days, for they bring to the quest for entertainment the flurried zeal that directs their businesses. In the beetling tenement houses they set their gramophones buzzing. In the mission halls venturesome voices lift the bathos of hymn-tunes to tragedy. From dim-lit bars the debilitated music of electric pianos brings ill-tidings of the search for gaiety; and above them all blares the band of the Salvation Army, strenuously wanton.

In a minor street of this district stood once a small shop with dim, reticent windows. Through these dusty windows sniggering boys would peer, and would nudge one another with furtive comment. The stock, dusty as the windows, seemed to have been thrown together by disdainful hands. There were faded photographs of monster-limbed actresses, in tights; a few books in paper covers, with titles matching the maladroit archness of the photographs; some bottles of scent with variegated labels; and little packets of toilet accessories. The ill-informed might have assumed, from the style and condition of the display, that the owner was letting his business run to ruin; while, in fact, he was doing very well. The goods in his window were not exposed for sale; they were a nod and a wink to the knowing ones that he had other tricks up his sleeve.

The shop bore no name on the front, but it was known to be the property of one Mr. Bronsden. He was a most worthy man. He kept himself *to* himself; and in England there is no more certain way of winning the respect of one's neighbours. He was a large man. His visage was sour; his complexion sanguine. His head was thatched with a mass of beer-coloured hair. His clothes and linen were always soiled, and he kept himself in tune with them, and walked with humility in side streets. Sour as his visage was, he could, on occasion, be jocose, and was so with esteemed customers; but jocosity came heavily from him, and his jokes were as sour and muddy as the lips over which they crawled.

This Bronsden owned, besides a comfortable little business, a wife. Few people had seen her. Few people indeed had even had sight of his private apartments. He was not a man who took pride or joy in his possessions. Though the wife was a recent acquisition, he took less account of her than some of his customers took of their home-made rabbit-hutches. Perhaps he was justified, for he had picked her off the streets. This is an action whose merit cannot be denied, for he found her when she had been but a few days in that situation, and, by his intervention, she was snatched from its attendant calamities. Beaten and broken she was wandering about the streets, when he came across her, and listened perfunctorily to her bitter words that were half appeal and half defiance.

Without any clear motive, he gave her shelter. Then he dismissed the old woman who played at attending him and robbed him of food and money, and installed Hetty in her place, and married her. The contract was plainly set forth; she entered his establishment as indoor servant, with duties, personal cash allowance, household allowance, and reasonable freedom of movement. Her position only differed from that of the ordinary domestic help by her being joined in holy matrimony to her employer: a rite upon which he had insisted so that she should be his fixed property.

Now should she have been proud of the dignity conferred upon her—a wastrel of the alleys; and for a few weeks she was. Then, being a servant in a good home ceased to content her. She wanted to stir delight in the muffled heart of Bronsden, and found that it was not in her power to do so. In her company, or without it, he was passive; her fluttering gesture and gamesome eye drew no response or quickening of the blood from him. He accepted her, as he accepted his pipe. Yet beauty rested in her weary face and her flowing figure, and she knew it and longed for its recognition. Because he was oblivious of her charms, she began to hate him; and because, to her honest mind, this neglect afforded no proper reason for hatred, she began to cast about for a reason.

She soon found one. Her distaste for her situation developed rapidly. I think she was not a woman of normal sensibilities. Though he was a strong, silent man, she could not reverence him. Though he was hard and heavy with his tongue, she did not admire the brute. She was foolish enough to want things to which she was not entitled: gentle hands, and respect, and little courtesies. Bronsden looked down to her from stony heights, but she did not look up to him. He had taken her from the streets in his big, abstracted way, on her first journey of misery, and had made her respectable. He had given her money for frocks and chocolates and knick-knacks. By Shadwell standards, he was the perfect husband. He was kind, in his aloof way, and occasionally sportive. She was indeed in a position to be envied. But . . . he was her rescuer, her benefactor. By all human ideas he was entitled to her gratitude and her service. In the eyes of the world she was deep in his debt. It was this fact that bit and burned her heart night and day. Herein she found good and sufficient reason for hatred.

In a room at the rear of his shop, looking on to a blank wall, he had fixed a laboratory, and there he toiled by day and increased the wadded brown smell of Shadwell as he compounded his dreadful medicines and surgical goods. To the shop would come often men of horrid aspect and slinking demeanour. They would murmur diffident words to Bronsden and would follow him through the living-room to the laboratory at the back; and there the two would remain in murmurous confabulation, with interjected sniggers. And in the living-room Hetty would sit and feed upon her hate.

Now all men are not so impervious to the graces of woman as this Bronsden. Tom the Toff was an inflammable young man; what is known, in certain circles, as a warm member. One glance from bright eyes would set him alight. He was as combustible as powder. And when, one morning, he passed Hetty in St. George's, her eyes applied the match. He followed her. He noted where she lived, and hung about each morning to watch for her appearance on the street with market basket. Time was his own; for he was Tom the Toff, a free-lance, who worked West End crowds for purses and handbags. He had an easy conquest. She was as ripe for the bold smile of this debonair philanderer as he for her sidelong glances.

He found early occasion for visiting the morose Bronsden in the way of business. He had a long talk with Bronsden. He told a tale, and listened to Bronsden expatiating on the merits of his remedies. Then he mentioned casually that he had a good deal of business in the West End; it might be worth Bronsden's considering whether he, Tom the Toff,

could work an agency for him among West End
gentlemen. This proposal Bronsden considered, and
it became necessary that Tom the Toff should visit
the shop many times for conferences and discussion
of terms. Within a week, Tom the Toff's presence
in the shop was accepted as casually as the presence
of a partner.

And Hetty no more sulked and gnawed herself
in the living-room. A light step on the threshold of
the shop filled her with music and laughter. Youth
leapt to youth. And when Bronsden was busy in
the laboratory, and could not be disturbed, there
were delicious minutes when they stood in each
other's presence, and looked and talked—oh, any
kind of talk, but a very special kind of look. It was
inevitable that she should turn to him. For he had
nothing to give her, in the way of material comforts.
His West End raids were intermittent, and yielded
a precarious income. It was, this time, for her, to
give; and she gave him with both hands the gift of
her love.

Tom the Toff felt the frigid atmosphere with
which Bronsden filled the house, and knew its effect
on a limber-hearted girl. At first, in her presence,
he was shy and diffident, dropping his easy, nonchalant air, and becoming awkward. By this Hetty
knew that their hearts were beating in tune, and by
exquisite gesture and significant attitude, sharper
messengers than any words, they made mutual dis-

covery. The barriers went down, then; and they discoursed freely, as though there were no Bronsden bulking between them.

But Bronsden was still there. Others knew it, if Tom and Hetty forgot it. Tom's father knew it, and said so.

"Wodyeh think yer up to?" he would inquire. "Eh? Going into business as a dealer in trouble— or what? This kind o' thing's going to be a lot o' use to you, ain't it? Messin' yesself up with another chap's wife. And what a wife! Yeh know where 'e found 'er, doncher? Remember I'm yer father. I seen more o' the world'n what you 'ave Besides, there's 'im. 'E ain't a man what says much, but, begor, I wouldn't like to be on the wrong side of 'im. Them quiet kind, when they breaks out, they breaks out. And Gawd 'elp the one they breaks on."

But Tom paid little heed to dad's garrulous admonitions. He had heard of dreadful things happening to other people, but it had never seemed likely that dreadful things could happen to him.

"I warn yeh!" went on dad. "I warn yeh. If anything comes o' this, yeh can't say I 'aven't warned yeh."

"No, yer right there," replied the respectful son. "I couldn't truthfully say that, considering yer at it morning and night. Yeh got a nice pleasant voice, dad, but I wonder yeh don't sometimes get a bit tired of 'earing it. I do."

In the living-room at evenings, Hetty would be notably vivacious and happy-eyed. Springtide hung about her and moved with her; but the saturine Bronsden ate his supper and saw nothing. Until, reckoning too boldly on his obtuseness, Tom the Toff presented Hetty with a yellow silk scarf And Hetty, drunk with glamour, wore it.

At supper on the night of its presentation, Bronsden noticed it. Only deliberately could he have ignored it. It was a brilliant yellow hue, with a long silk fringe. With it about her shoulders Hetty could have been picked up at a mile distant.

"Where d'you get that?"

"Get what?"

"That scarf you got on."

"Oh, that?" airily. "Oh, Tom the Toff give me that."

"Tom the Toff gave you that? Whaffor?"

"Oh, just a sort of present, like. Sort of acknowledgment of what he's made out of placing your stuff up there."

"Give it to me," he said gently.

"What?"

"Take it off and give it to me."

"Whaffor?"

His eyes snapped. His voice rose. "Never mind what for. Give it to me."

"Of course I shan't. It was given to me."

He stretched a hand, and spoke gently. "Give me that scarf."

"Shan't."

In one movement his great form rose from the table and came to her. With a twitch of the hand he snatched it from her shoulders, crumpled it into a ball, and thrust it into his pocket.

"Understand, girl, that you're my wife. I don't let my wife have presents from other men. See? Understand that?"

Hetty shrank back. The shock of his action had staggered her. "Wha—wha—wha——" Then tears came, and sobs, and she beat herself with her fists, unable to beat him. Then words came.

"You beast! You brute. Gimme back my scarf. I'm not your slave. I ain't going to be crushed like this. You stifle me. You treat me like dirt. Gimme my scarf."

"My wife won't take presents from other men. Understand?"

"No, I don't. If I am your wife, I'm a human being. I got a right to live, ain't I? Oh, I know. . . . You think 'cos you played the Good Samaritan, you can do what you like with me. But you can't. You can't. I'll show you you can't."

"Now, Hetty, why talk like that? It isn't true. You know it isn't. Have I ever once thrown it up to you—about where I found you? Have I?"

She knew he had not, and the fact angered her more. She went on in a torrent of words:

"You crush me. You never speak a word to me. One wouldn't know you got a tongue. It's like living with the deaf and dumb. You—you—you're fat, y—you're old. You make me sick the way you treat me. 'Cos you're dull yesself, you want to make me as dull. But I won't be dull. There! I'll do what I like. I bin a good wife to you—you can't say I ain't—and I alwis looked after you proper. Why shouldn't I talk to Tom the Toff, if I want to? Where's the harm in that? If you won't talk to me, you can't stop me talking to someone else who's— who's bright—and—and lively and—and got a bit of go in him."

"Now, Hetty. Now, girl. What's the matter with me, exactly? Where am I wrong? He sought to soothe her with his voice, tolerantly, as one soothes a querulous child. It was the wrong way.

"Oh, shut up! You're *all* wrong. You—your ways and your manners and——" She knew what she wished to say, the fine distinctions of character she wished to draw; but her range of words was restricted. "Anyway, I'll please myself. A wife's supposed to be mistress of her own home, ain't she? I'm like a kitchen-maid here. I ain't hardly able to call me soul me own. But you may as well know that I've asked Tom the Toff to supper to-morrow night."

His manner changed from the soothing to the ruffled. His face began to close up. "Oh, you have, have you? And what have I got to say about it?"

"Don't know and don't care. Gimme my scarf."

"Tom the Toff won't come to supper to-morrow night."

"He will!" she screamed.

"He won't. He won't come into this shop again." He came closer to her. "You can assert your right to please yourself in some other way. Not this way. Understand? I don't coop you up or stifle you. I've only tried to protect you against yourself— against your own ignorance. If I hadn't, you'd soon a-been sliding back to where I found you. And, Hetty, don't try any tricks with me. See? Two or three people have found out that it don't pay to play tricks with me."

She glared back at him, and saw something in his face that made her suddenly afraid. "You talk to me as if I was a kid!" she protested sullenly. "Why can't you treat me properly?"

"Have I ever ill-treated you?"

"Not the way you mean. But you done it by taking all the life out o' me. By taking no notice of me—not more'n if I was that table. Gimme my scarf."

"I shall not give you that scarf. I tell you—if you want to assert your right to please yourself, do it some other way."

"I don't want no other way!" She ground the words from her teeth, and then was sorry. Her secret was out. She knew that, from the dull spark that glowed in his eye.

He regarded her intently; then said, quietly, as one dismissing a trifle: "I shall not give you that scarf."

She glowered, finished with words and without capacity for action. He returned to his chair, and relapsed into gloom. And for the rest of the evening they sat in frightful silence, while he followed with his eyes her smallest movement.

When she moved to clear the table, he rose, and went into his laboratory. She watched him go with hateful eyes. She saw him no more until midnight, when he came out, looking tired and bent. He moved about the kitchen. She continued to read the serial in *The Sunday Fireside*.

"It's getting late," he said, after a long silence. "You coming to bed?"

"Not yet. I want to finish this."

He hung about for some minutes; then went upstairs. The moment she heard the click of the bedroom door, she dropped *The Sunday Fireside*, and got up.

"The beast! Treats me like a kid, he does. I won't be treated like this. I wonder if he's got it on him. Or whether he's hidden it."

She lit a candle, and went into the laboratory.

Here she pottered, nosing around, pulling things about, opening drawers, humming and fretting to herself. At last she found it. He had screwed it tight into a ball and had thrust it into an old tin box. She snatched it savagely away, and thrust it inside her corsage.

"Ha! Mr. Clever Dick. I'm as smart as you."

Bitter fury, loose and without dignity, possessed her. Her mind was yapping at his, and snarling and grimacing like a whipped child. His suave demeanour under the quarrel had increased her hatred of him. She knew that she had dropped all grace and had become ludicrous in her rage, and she envied him his self-sufficiency. But she thrilled at the fact that she had retrieved the scarf, and this lent her some pride.

She went up to bed swaggering, and no word passed between them that night or next morning. He shut himself in his laboratory till noon. Then he came out for dinner, and over the meal broke the silence.

"Look here, Hetty, we can't go on like this. It's too silly. If you want Tom the Toff to supper, he can come. And anybody else you like to invite. I don't want you to think I crush you. If it's company and society you want, I know I'm not very gay. So if it'll make you happy to have him, have him. Peace and quietness is all I want."

She looked up, surprised at this sudden change,

and found him regarding her gravely, scrutinising her, passing veiled eyes over her person. She was not ready for this surrender. She did not know how to accept it.

"Well, I do want company and all that," she said lamely.

"I know. I know I'm old and—— You please yourself."

"Oh, well——"

And so the quarrel was healed, and Tom the Toff came to supper. With that supper in the back room her desire for love and gaiety ended. Tom the Toff arrived on time, and found the table laid with cold meat, salad, beer, fruit, cheese. Bronsden was out, and he and Hetty snatched a few rapturous minutes; but before she could tell him of what had passed last night, Bronsden returned, bearing a tin of salmon and a bottle of whisky, as a friendly addition to the table. He seemed downcast, preoccupied; but he greeted Tom the Toff with his usual detached affability, and inquired what he had backed that day.

"Got the tin-opener Hetty? he growled.

She brought it, and he set to work on the tin. It was a tough one, and awkward to hold, tipping up when he pressed on its edge.

"Dammit! Just a minute, Tom, will yeh? This is as hard as steel. Can't get the point in. Hold it firm, will yeh, while I have another try."

Tom came to the table, and placed both hands on the tin, holding it firm. They stood close together, their heads meeting, and in silence Bronsden pressed on the cutter to drive its point through the tin. Then the silence was broken by a high ripping squeak. The cutter had slipped along the edge of the tin.

With a sharp "Ow!" Tom's hand flashed to his mouth.

"I say, old man!" Bronsden stood, holding the cutter, his attitude one of much concern. "I say, I'm awfully sorry. The cutter slipped. Damn the thing."

"Oh, it's all right," said Tom. "It's nothing." But when he took his hand from his mouth the blood ran around his wrist and down his fingers from an angry, jagged wound. It came pouring out to the tablecloth, and down that to the floor. It was no common wound.

Immediately Hetty swerved from the side-table, where she had been cutting bread.

"Oh, Tom!"

"Bind it up!" snapped Bronsden. "Quick!" Hetty turned about the room with hands out for bandage. Then they flew to her breast, and out came the yellow scarf.

Bronsden had gone to his chair, and sat back, calmly. At this sudden action his big head nodded in two minute movements.

"Where d'you get that?" he said quietly. "I thought I took it away from you."

She made no answer, but twisted the scarf into a bandage.

"Did you steal that from my room?"

"Mind your own business."

"You're not to use it," he said, in even tones.

"I shall do as I please."

"Hetty, I tell you not to use it. Get the towel."

"Oh, shut up. Can't you see Tom's bleeding?"

"Very well."

She fussed over Tom, tender-wise, maternally, and wound the scarf tightly about his wrist. Then she forced him to a chair, and herself sat down. She sat down with a flirt of defiance too strongly marked to carry conviction of self-possession. This accident had given her opportunity for open challenge of this man's bondage. She sat upright, her attitude expressing: "Well, and what now?"

Bronsden poured two glasses of whisky, and passed one to Tom. "I'm sorry, old man," he growled. "Awfully sorry. Those damn tin-openers. I always said they were dangerous. Keep your arm up. Hetty'll have to cut your meat for you now, and feed you."

Suddenly, Tom emitted a gasp—another gasp—then a scream. He pressed his free hand to the damaged wrist, and bent forward. His teeth were set close, his face twisted in pain.

"What is it?" Hetty cried.

"Oo, it's burning!" he gasped. "Burning like hell. 'Strewth!" Hetty came to him, in agitation, but as she reached him he leapt up, and dashed himself against the wall, and screamed. Oo, God, I can't stand it!" He tore at the scarf and unwound it from his wrist. "It's going all over me. Oh, Hetty, what you done to me? What you done to me? I'm going all funny. When you put that scarf on it started. Hetty!"

He sank back to the leather sofa, and Hetty rushed to him. She grabbed the whisky glass, and held some to him. She dithered. And, as she hung over him, uncertain what to do, unable to do one thing by thinking of others, she was suddenly seized by a feeling that something dreadful had entered the room. Involuntarily she turned her head and glanced about her. Then she saw the thing that had entered the room. Bronsden sat immovable in his chair; but on his face was a wry, dark smile.

"What is it?" she cried vaguely. "What's the matter?"

"Nothing."

"What you smiling at?"

"Nothing. You know, I *told* you not to use that scarf."

Tom the Toff dropped like a log on the floor. She looked at him and at the yellow scarf and at the door leading to the dreadful laboratory, and back at her husband. She went and stood over him.

"You damn devil—wotter you done?"

Quivering, she struck him in the face. But he only smiled. And, though she struck him again and again, he still smiled.

A GAME OF POKER

— II —

A GAME OF POKER

A S Archie Plumpton, known to his circle as
Plum-plum, stepped from the glare of the Blue
Lantern into the melting radiance that it diffused,
and from that into the inhospitable darkness of
Poplar, three men with flat faces and long eyes crept
from their several observation posts and followed
him. One walked behind him, one level with him
across the street, and one a few paces ahead. From
a side street ambled a small hooded van drawn by
a pony. This, at a discreet distance, joined the
party. Plum-plum walked upright, whistling to himself, one hand in trousers pocket, the other swinging free. The others walked silently, with an air
of abstraction and concern with personal affairs.

It was a warm night of summer, and streets and
houses were stewing in a viscid heat. Plum-plum
strolled airly down East India Dock Road, glad of
the slight breeze that wandered from the river and
oblivious of the peril that moved busily with him.
Certainly he had asked for the trouble that was
coming to him; for, if it is injudicious to be funny

with a policeman, it is more than folly to meddle with the affairs of a Chinese brotherhood. Plum-plum had done no less than thrust hand and foot into the intimate affairs of the Azure Dragon Tong.

Word had come to him, some while ago, of an accumulation of carven vessels, gems and other objects that please the eye of the connoisseur, which lay at a certain house in Poplar High Street, next door to which he had sometimes played at puckapoo. He had seen the stuff through the window of the front room, and had almost cried with professional vexation at seeing such a haul placed within finger-reach, to be obtained without the smallest exercise of technical skill or finesse. It almost seemed beneath his position to take them.

But he did take them. He walked in one afternoon, at the hour of sleep, and took them away in a bag, and passed them to his nearest friend and adorer, Flash Florrie. He thought he had done only what he had done many times before—intervened between police and receiver in the matter of the bunce. He did not know that he had administered a dreadful affront to the most powerful Tong in Limehouse.

He was soon made to know. Cold anger held the Azure Dragon Tong at the discovery of this insolence. It quickly became known about the district that it was Plum-plum's work and the boys, once their envy of his slimness had passed, talked of it

with appreciation and delight. They could understand the delicious impudence of it, and admire ac-
cordingly; and Plum-plum became a public hero.
But the Tong held a council to decide what proceed-
ings should be taken against him. The president
asked who accused Plum-plum, and two stepped
forward and repeated the street-corner stories. To
these two was assigned the duty of entering the
house of Plum-plum and making an exact search for
the treasure, at whatever cost to their persons or
their liberties. This was done, and failure reported.
Plum-plum came home one night and found his three
rooms ransacked and torn apart; and he smiled.
The Tong did not smile. Another meeting was
held, and it was decided that Plum-plum himself
must be secretly apprehended, and made to discover
the whereabouts of their property, and, after suit-
able punishment, surrender it.

At least (they held among themselves) if we do
not by the means we are about to employ recover
our property—at least the Englishman will receive
a lesson that it is unwise to interfere with our affairs.
He shall be an example to others.

So the three men and the hooded van, now dog-
ging Plum-plum, were engaged in carrying out the
decision of the council. And Plum-plum walked
carelessly, still bearing about him something of that
public glory with which his exploit had endued him.
He was a dexterous and versatile lad, and had been

desired by more than one gang, as partner. But he preferred to play a lone hand. He was not a crook by education or inclination. He would have liked to be a decent citizen, but found decent citizenship so dull. He had drifted into this game because he liked its soldier-of-fortune atmosphere, and because he was too wayward and impatient of hours, regulations and the petty bonds of legitimate business. He had found, too, on his preliminary flourish, that he had a marked aptitude for it; and every man likes to do the work that he can do really well and without conscious effort. He wore crime as a feather in his cap. He could appear in any society without crying at the top of his voice: "I'm a crook!" He could get away with a policeman's truncheon while being examined on suspicion. He could collect money for the missionaries with one hand and snaffle the donor's watch with the other. These were small tricks; he did not preen himself with them. It was the bigger things, calling for strategy, that afforded him delight. But he had never tackled the Chinese before, and he had yet to learn that his tricks with them were as paper swords before steel weapons.

To the end of East India Dock Road he went, and, at the Iron Bridge at Canning Town, he crossed suddenly, and passed into the void of Plaistow Marsh and its meagre lamps and its waist-high mist. He was going towards Beckton, where lodged Flash

Florrie. As he entered the Marsh the three fol-
lowers drew together at a corner and exchanged,
tacitly, emotions of satisfaction. A lonely, lugubrious bell announced ten o'clock, and the notes floated
miserably about the waste. But Plum-plum was not
conscious of his surroundings. His eyes were fixed
on the line of lights that made the horizon, and he
strode with nonchalant step, his thoughts hovering
amiably about the bright person of Flash Florrie
and her sturdy, tree-like beauty.

But midway across the Marsh a sudden misstep
of one of the Chinks came sharply to his ears. Momentarily suspicion entered his mind, and drove out
the bees and butterflies that fluttered there. He
stood still, and heard no other step, and knew that
he was being followed. This was nothing new.
He was often shadowed by plain-clothes men, and
could always feel their attentions and comport himself circumspectly. But plain-clothes men do not
walk about in slippers, and the step he had heard
was a slippered step. As he stood there, a deeper
sense of imminent personal danger grew within him;
and, even as he speculated upon its nature, it arrived.

The struggle was brief. He fought hard for a
few moments, and caught a glimpse of close, round
faces and long eyebrows. Then something was
pressed against his nose and he fell solidly among
them. From the distance the pony-cart came to

them; and into this, and its litter of greengrocer's baskets and potato sacks, he was bundled. The three companions followed him, and the cart moved forward.

Slowly they crossed the Marsh, while Plum-plum slept stupidly. On the farther side they chose by-ways. They rumbled through alleys of ebony darkness, whose very noises had the hard quality of ebony; and through streets parallel with the placid river, about which dodged innumerable nimble tugs. Not a word passed between the company; a profound, uneasy silence held the van.

And so they came to the little lost colony of Cyprus. Cyprus is a frigid, dusty region where the four winds and their branch winds meet, and where the sun comes seldom. Its houses are square brick boxes, at whose doors squat or lounge the docksmen. About the stony streets the children gambol day and night; and from slatternly windows peer the women. In this corner, where the lips of the Thames dribble into little purposeless canals, silence cannot live. The Chinks had chosen their location well, for the business they had in hand. From year to year, hammer, crane, syren, hooter and bell perform their rough, unceasing music; iron against iron, steel against steel, with a chorus of nail and rivet; and through the night the shunted trucks make a melancholy fugue. The glum streets and forlorn shops make dreadful efforts to assert the presence of humanity, but Work prevails: one long-drawn hysteria of toil; one everlasting hosanna of noise. Men come and go in worried, clamant haste; and through the stupendous turmoil tramps and destroyers crawl with an air of scornful idleness.

To a narrow street of warehouses in this ill-named Cyprus came the greengrocer's van. It stopped at a tall door which was immediately opened, revealing a steep flight of stone steps. Up these steps Plum-plum was carried; and thence to a room on the top landing. The room was an unused room, plainly arranged for the occasion. The boards were bare; the plaster of the walls had fallen in a mess of chips; and the windows, which looked into the chilly face of Cyprus, were heavily swathed with matting. Four lighted candles in bottles stood on a deal box. Round the fireplace stood a screen, and in the grate a clear fire was burning.

The three men placed Plum-plum on the floor, and one brought sturdy cord and bound his wrists and feet. Another brought a bucket of water, and the water was thrown about his head and throat. After some seconds he opened his eyes and looked about him. He raised his head, and tried to move, and found he could only roll. He rolled over and looked up, and saw four silent yellow men regarding him. He looked long at them, slowly coming back from his deep sleep. Then he understood, and spoke.

"Well, Oswald, what's the game? What-um you fella want to do me?"

One, who seemed to be the leader of the party, and was addressed as Ah Kang, spoke without moving. He spoke as one delivering a functional address; in the cool, sleek tones of a chairman of a company meeting.

"I so sorry disturb you, misteh. I lika little talk with you 'bout t'ings you steal from my flen in Poplar. Huh? I ting we talk more flenly lika diss."

"Oh? I don't call *this* friendly." Plum-plum indicated the cord about his arms. "I could talk better if you untied me."

Ah Kang gave a little indrawing of the breath, as one appreciating a jocularity. "Ho yess? We talk 'bout t'ings you steal us."

"No savee, Oswald."

Ah Kang's eyes snapped, but he did not move. "Wantum jewels," he said in peremptory tone. "You no go 'way less we get jewels."

"No can. Ain't gottum jewels."

Ah Kang ignored the denial. "What you do withum jewels?"

"No can tell. Never seen 'em."

"You talk no-truth." Ah Kang stepped forward, and motioned to the others. They went to Plum-plum, and dragged him to a sitting posture, and pulled aside the screen.

"You see-um fire?" asked Ah Kang.

Plum-plum looked at it, and saw. "No can."
You give back jewels. You tellum where they go.
And it will be betteh—much betteh. If you no tell
—prap fire 'e mek you tell. Huh?"

Plum-plum looked at the unblinking fire and the
shaded faces about him, and felt suddenly sick. He
thought of Flash Florrie, under whose bed rested
the property. They would not release him until the
treasure was in their possession, and if he told them,
he must remain in their custody while they went to
her home. By what method they would recover
their property from her, and what penalty they
would inflict upon her for her part in the affront,
he did not like to think. He jerked his head at
them.

"Look 'ere, if you think you can muck about like
this with Englishmen, you're dam fella well mistaken—see? If you don't let me go pretty quick,
there'll be heap trouble for you—and all the rest of
your bunch. So I tell yeh! Stop this foolery plenty
dam quick and untie me. See!"

Ah Kang stood over him. "You tellum where
jewels are."

"You go to hell!"

Ah Kang permitted himself to smile, and flicked
his fingers at the others. The screen was drawn
around the fire, and Plum-plum heard the clatter of
metal instruments. Next moment he was flung
down, and his coat, shirt and collar were ripped

from his shoulders by a sharp knife. He lay quiescent. To struggle was futile. To shout for help he knew was vain. Where he was he did not know; but he knew enough of the Chinks to be sure that, having planned this business, they would have been careful to carry him where cries for help would pass unheeded.

Ah Kang spoke again in suave tones: "You tellum where jewels are?"

Plum-plum spat at him, then shut his teeth and looked away. From time to time the others moved about, nodding among themselves and exchanging smiles that were frightfully discordant with the business in hand. When Ah Kang reproved the smiles they went behind the screen, and Plum-plum heard them murmuring and grunting together. He heard the crackling of the fire, the rattle of coke as they replenished it; and he was conscious of the increased warmth which the screen could not effectually enclose.

There are some things before which no man can retain his faith; to which the body must surrender, however steadfast the spirit; and Plum-plum knew that sooner or later he must give way. No creature can endure physical pain beyond a certain point, and that point is determined not by courage but by sensibility. The "strong" man is a creature of blunted nerves and brute skin; yet even he has his breaking-point. Plum-plum knew that his breaking-point was very near. He seemed to see through the screen the glowing fire, white-hot, and the preparations of which it was the centre and he the object. He felt already the touch of hot iron; but, until he could endure no more, he would not speak. He did not suffer fear, but he did suffer a physical nausea that almost drained him of resistance.

He knew he would have to speak before he left that room—in one minute or two minutes or five minutes; yet the spirit that had carried him so aptly through so many delicate engagements closed his lips. He could not speak now, while he was in full control of his faculties. He felt that to do so would be to turn himself from man into a mere husk covered with everlasting self-loathing. Afterwards— after *that*—he would not be himself; and neither words nor actions would carry any sting of self-reproach.

"Dissa pokeh prap 'e mek you talk, huh?"

"You go to hell!"

From the streets, the strident but desirable streets, came distantly an organ's titillating music; its exuberant vulgarity overriding the stealthy crackling of the fire and the subdued movements of the hidden Chinks. Then Ah Kang uttered a curt word. Plum-plum was rolled over, and one pressed heavily on his neck. From behind the screen came another with a poker, its point glowing red. Plum-plum heard his slippered step, and, though he could not see, he could follow his steady approach; he could follow the movement of the extended arm; he could feel the glowing thing upon his back; he could see the horrid mark that it would leave. Ah Kang spoke again, and the man with the poker made a slow, drawing movement with it across the shoulders of Plum-plum.

A rendering shriek came from the victim, and his whole body heaved in a spasm. Ah Kang made a movement, and the man with the poker stood aside.

"You tellum where jewels are now, or——"

Plum-plum made no sound.

"Huh? You no had-um plenty lesson? We try again."

Again the poker was drawn across his shoulders, slowly, lingeringly. But this time it brought no cry, no movement. The four men exchanged glances. Ah Kang moved to Plum-plum and rolled him over. He placed a hand on his breast, and looked up with an expressionless face, while his mind suffered wonder, perplexity, anger. They would not now find the jewels. Plum-plum was dead.

"He dead," said Ah Kang stupidly.

"Dead?" The others echoed him stupidly. They said it again among themselves, and all looked stupidly at the poker. The man who held it was twisting it and snapping it to pieces in his hands— a wooden stick, painted to resemble steel, and, and its point, painted a shrill scarlet.

So they stood, dumb, anxious, impotent, until one of them went again to Plum-plum to touch him and turn him over; and at the same moment he sprang far back from the body with a high scream and a trembling arm outstretched to Plum-plum's back.

"Hee-yah!"

Across the shoulders was a long brown mark— the seared trail of a red-hot poker. A tense and throbbing silence enveloped them—a silence of superstitious alarm; and in the close heat of that room they drew together, shivering.

KATIE THE KID

III

KATIE THE KID

KATIE THE KID was none of your rapturous,
languishing, kiss-me girls. She was a Stunner.
She was a Spanker. She was a jazz of a girl. She
knew Shadwell, whose dun light was the first she
saw, as few people know their native place. She
knew it inside out. Many times had she taken it to
pieces, that she might find out what made it work;
and when she thus tampered with it, she seldom put
it back correctly: there was usually a cog missing
when she had finished with it. And for perhaps
three or six months the proper motions of Shadwell would be retarded, while the cog picked oakum
or made sacks under State supervision.

Yes, Katie the Kid was a nark. She was by no
means your common nark, who is a poor, spiritless,
servile fellow, cringing to his employers and going
in bodily fear of his victims. She had the game
well taped. She knew all the tricks of the times,
and her ample sleeve held others, not yet of the
times. In heart and sinew she was concrete. She
took money from the gangs, and money from the

police, and sold the plans of each to the other. She walked about St. George Street and its cowering alleys with the tread of the conqueror. She strode. She moved with the sturdy grace of a steel ship, and her long, lusty limbs swayed forward as though making way through advancing seas. A nest of dense, crisp curls was built against her big, bright face, from which glowed defiant eyes of jet. She wore the best feathers and drank the best beer, and put a little bit by.

And then the big fool fell in love.

She fell in love with Freddie Frumkin, who was beginning to be known to vigilant sportsmen as a likely lad. She first saw him at a series of trial contests at a little boxing hall on the south of the river; and the lithe, quivering figure and the shining white skin of him, as he danced about the ring and received blow after blow with game nonchalance, set her too a-dancing and a-quivering, and filled her with an emotion which she hardly understood. It was new to her. In the eighth round he was knocked out; and though, hitherto, she had felt only contempt for the defeated in any kind of contest, this knockout blow went straight to her heart. It first cracked—this concrete heart of hers—then swiftly melted. That night she took his image to her pillow, and lay awake in blessed brooding, and knew that love had come to her; and being, with all her

tricks, fiercely modest in physical matters, she was
suddenly abashed and humiliated.

Soon, diffidently, by means which every woman
can employ, she sought his acquaintance, and won it.
By the same means she made him know the state
of her feelings; and he—well, he was a big, healthy
boy, and when he looked upon this big, healthy girl
and heard her words, the thing was done. Thereafter they went about together and agreed in everything. At all his contests Katie the Kid was present,
as near the ring as she could get, to exhort him to
victory and blight his opponent to ineptitude.

Glibly, as one long skilled in misrepresentation,
she told him her story: how she was without parents,
and worked in a cigarette factory near the Tower;
how she lived alone, and spent her spare time in
reading books borrowed from the Free Library, and
never went about with boys, or strolled along her
local Monkey's Parade, deeming such doings unworthy any self-respecting girl. Whereat Freddie
glowed, and wondered that so sweet and gentle a
girl should have seen anything in a rough young
pug like himself, or should even suffer his company.
He told her so, and said that she made him feel
ashamed, and made him want to do better and bigger things. You know how it is with your first girl.

On this, Katie began to think. She began to think
about herself, and her stock of self-esteem dropped
sharply. If she inspired Freddie Frumkin with a

desire for nobler ways of life, he in turn inspired her with yearnings. He was so clean and cool and simple that she discovered in herself a desire for clean and cool and simple things. She tried suddenly to cut the nark business and the secret commission business. To the loud derision of the Geranium Street police station she started the follow-the-gleam business. As no man is so ardent a teetotaller as your reclaimed dipsomaniac, so with Katie the Kid. She placed herself in the hands of the local Settlement Workers, and set about looking for steady and decent employment. It was even said that she was to attend the open-air mission meetings at the corner of Love Lane on Wednesday evenings; but the police prevented this last indecency. Such backsliding didn't suit them. They made a grand remonstrance.

"Dammit," said the sergeant, "what the hell's she want to turn pious for? With anybody else it'd a-bin all to the good for us. But *her!* We can't get on without her. We gotter git her back some'ow."

They did. Remonstrances failed, but economic pressure succeeded. Her savings were soon exhausted; and wherever the local Settlement Workers went among employers, with stories of her industry and moral rectitude, they found that the police had been before them. There was no job for Katie the Kid. So, quietly, she took up again her secret duties. Fortunately, Freddie's home was by Bermondsey Wall, and was severed from hers by the river. Gossip of the North side seldom reaches the South, and they had no common friends. Thus she was able to continue as a nark in Shadwell, while in Bermondsey she was a factory hand with yearnings towards self-culture.

Three evenings a week, when Freddie was not engaged, she would go to him, and they would walk comfortably together in the flare and glitter of Jamaica Road, where the girls parade with frolicsome frocks and gleeful eyes; or down the more modest byways where lights are few. It was just after her return to her old employment that Freddie spoke casually of his need of a punching-ball. He was not yet promising enough to attract gifts of equipment from backers, and he had only the gymnasium at the boxing booth in which to train, which was a damn nuisance. A punching-ball, to be fixed in the back-yard of his home, would be the very thing. But they were damn expensive.

Katie pondered the idea at night, and she guessed why he could not purchase the ball. There had been rides on the bus on Sundays, some visits to the local music hall, and a little gilt cross and chain for her sapling neck. From her there had been as yet no gift: her savings were gone, and for the moment crime was short, and there was little coming in from the police. She went home that night to devise means of raising money and to study sporting papers for some hint as to the price of punching-balls.

Next day something came her way. In the street, local gossip made much of the theft of many rolls of cloth from a dry-goods warehouse. Thieves and cloth were well away, and the police were "pursuing inquiries." The sergeant sought Katie, met her in the street, flicked an eye at her and disappeared down an alley. She followed him.

"Ah, Katie—just looking for you. Got a job for you. You heard about this cracking of Higginses' place. Well, there's four dozen rolls of cloth gone—good stuff, too. We're stuck on it, for the moment. We're watching all the boys, but haven't got anything so far. Now, it's up to you. Higginses are offering a reward, and if you can put us on to the stuff or the men, you'll do yourself a bit o' good. I dessay there might be a couple o' quid in it for you. See? So put yer back into it."

"Right-o! I'll have a look round."

That day her mind ran on rolls of cloth and punching-balls. A couple o' quid. That ought to be sufficient for the purpose. So she set to work, the punching-ball suspended before her, with gentle thoughts flitting about it, while, in the recesses of her mind, the rolls of cloth covered some crushed, but still moving instincts. It was her first job since her reformation; and soon the old fever of the hunt

crept into her veins. It ran with her blood, and set
a pace; and the thrills that some find in strong
drink and some in sex and some in works of art
coursed about her shoulders.

Into the dark places of Shadwell she went; into
places where discreet men would not go; into places
of dirt and crawling beastliness. She went, too, into
bright places; into well-kept taverns, where men
were clean and flashily dressed. She hung about
highways and alleys. She gathered a word here,
a half-sentence there. She drank heavily with old
acquaintance and casual company. It was Dick the
Duke who set her on the way, with a shrug and a
few words.

"Getting about a bit to-day, ain't you, Katie?
What's the game, eh? You ain't going to tell me
you're on Higginses' affair? Eh? Good lord!
Fancy wasting yer time on that. You're worth bet-
ter jobs than that. Blasted lot of amateurs.
They've hid it, kid. *Hid* it!"

Katie made no clear reply to his perfunctory
remarks, but stood him another drink and drank
with him; and had another at his shout. Then she
strolled idly away. There was but one place in
Shadwell where amateurs hid things, and to that
place she went. Near the old Basin, she stopped
at an open-air coffee caravanserai, labelled
"Jumbo's," which stood under an arch, backed
against the doors of a disused storage vault. She

took a cup of coffee here, and used her eyes. She made goo-goos at Jumbo, and chi-iked him.

"Got a new suit, eh, Jumbo? My word, we're coming it, ain't we? Nice bit o' cloth, too."

A minute movement at the corner of his lips on the word "cloth," which would have been unperceived by others, or have conveyed nothing if it had been perceived, satisfied Katie. She was watching for it.

She ambled back to Geranium Street.

"I found that bunce of Higginses."

"Good girl. You shall have a nice sweety for that. Where is it?"

"Old Jumbo's got it. In that vault behind 'is place. 'Tanyrate 'e knows all about it."

"Oho. We'll send round and have a little chit-chat with Jumbo."

"Right-o! I'll wait. When do I get the dough?"

"Just as soon as we confirm it, ducky."

The officer called for a plain-clothes man, and assigned him to a friendly cup of coffee with Jumbo. Within half-an-hour he returned.

"I seen Jumbo, and warned him. Same old Jumbo. Injured innocence. First, he didn't know nothing about it. Then minding it for some customers of his. However, I put the wind up him prop'ly. They're calling for the stuff to-night— or one or two of 'em are—and I got a list of all the names out of him. It's a gang of six, apparently. I got the names 'ere. I warned Jumbo extra special, and put it across him. Said we'd have him for a stretch if he so much as winked an eye. So if we wait till to-night we can catch 'em removing it, and then round up the others. Jumbo won't move at all—he's too fond of his own skin."

"Right-o! Well, we may as well have an observation man on there, in case. Get Gordon on to it."

"Satisfied?" asked Katie.

"Yes, kid, that's all right. Here you are. Now go and get yesself a good rump-steak, with lashings of onions—you look a bit all-gone."

She took the money, but her first thought was not of food, but of the shop in Cable Street where athletic goods were sold. To it she went, and returned with her purchase. In her one-room home she cooked herself a hotch-potch meal, with tea; and when she had eaten she straightened herself, and set out for Bermondsey.

During the walk her mind gambolled in pleasant pastures. She saw Freddie's strong white arms at work upon the punching-ball, and glowed with pride as she anticipated his raptures at the long-desired gift. They met near Cherry Gardens Pier, where it is dark, and at once his arms were about her, and his lips upon hers, while she fingered lovingly the blue scarf about his neck. Then they walked slowly towards Jamaica Road. Under the lamplight he noticed the unwieldy parcel she was carrying.

"What you got there, kid?"

"Aha! Never you mind. You wait and see."

He led her to the "Man in the Moon," kept by a friend of his, who allowed him the use of the back room, where were seats and a fire. He was in high feather. "Now, Katie, order what you like. I bin a bit short o' the ready lately, but I just clicked fer a bit from old Briggles, who's trying to get me a match with Dotty Jewett. I reckin I could settle 'im in three rounds if it comes orf. So 'ave just what yeh like." She chose a port-and-lemonade, and he ordered a dry-ginger for himself. "Now then, let's 'ave a button-hook at yer parcel."

Proudly she tossed it to him. "Open it."

He opened it. "Well, I'm damned! Now, Katie! Now who'd a-thought of you doing that? Now, reely! But, I say—— Well, well, well. And you bin an' bought this fer me? No, but—— Well, there! You didn't ought to 'ave, though. Reely, Katie, you didn't. They cost a lot o' money, I know. More'n you can prop'ly afford. You didn't—— Oh, you dear kid! If you ain't a real pal!" He tossed the ball to the ceiling, and caught it, and grinned broadly, and tossed it back again, then became serious.

"No, but, Katie—you shouldn't a-done it. You've 'ad to work damn 'ard fer this, I know. A lot of overtime and saving-up. Fancy you thinking all this of me, though. Just what I wanted, too. And from you! Katie—you think too much of me. I ain't 'alf good enough fer you. I don't deserve that a girl like you should think so much of me. I ain't worth you—your—love. I—— 'Ere—what's the matter? Katie!"

For suddenly Katie spluttered over her port, and burst into a howl of sobs, and big tears ran for the first time down those firm, dry cheeks.

"Why, Katie kid, what's up? There now—you bin overworking—that's what it is. You ain't bin feeding properly. You bin starving yesself to get this ball. 'Ere, I say—oh, Katie!"

"Oh, I can't keep it up no longer, Freddie. 'Tain't what you think. It's—it's me. It's—it's your—l-love. It's the way you think of me. I ain't worth it. I'm a beast. I'm a liar."

" 'Ere, don't be silly, kid." He spoke roughly, awkwardly. "Pull yesself together!"

"I can't. I can't keep it up no longer. It's no good. Not when you talk to me like you bin doing. You're so clean and strong and—and—right. And I'm—— I told you I worked in a cigarette factory, and kep' meself respectable. And it's all lies. I never bin in a factory. And I ain't respectable. Go away. Don't come near me. Lemme go 'ome. I didn't buy that ball by saving up or overtime at the factory. I'm—I'm a c-copper's nark. That's what I am. A dirty, sneaking copper's nark. That's what bought your punch-ball. Narking. It ain't fit for you to use. It's dirty. Chuck it away. And chuck me with it, fer making you love me and l-leading you on w-with l-lies."

She put her head to the table, and Freddie turned about the little room, shamed, apparently, at the sight of woman's distress; but his eyes were bright. He dug his hands deep into his pockets.

"Er—Katie?"

" 'M."

"You ain't telling me anything. I knew."

"You *knew?* Knew what?"

"What you was. I knew it before."

"*Knew?* When? Who told yeh?"

"I known it all along. From the first."

"You known it all along? And bin out wi' me, and kep' up wi' me? You? You let me go about wi' yeh, and said all those things to me, as though you meant 'em?"

"I did mean 'em. I do mean 'em."

"You—so clean and straight, going about wi' me, knowing what I was?"

" 'M. I knew you was a nark. But I didn't want you to know I knew in case I should lose yeh.

So I let you think I believed about the cigarette
factory. 'Cos——Katie——I see something fine about
you. About the way you loved me. I see you
wanted to be something better, cos' of me—like I
felt about you. I knew you tried to cut it out—
over in Shadwell. I 'eard all about it. And I knew
then that you was all right. And I loved you more
for it. Any feller would. And I says to meself—
she's straight, although she's bin a nark, and she
loves me, and as soon as I can get a bit together
she shall come out of it, and we'll make a fresh
start. That's what I said. And I ain't going to
throw you away. It's fer you to do the throwing.
Listen, Katie. I loved you, knowing what you was.
You loved me, thinking I was different from what
I was. What d'you think my job is?"

"Boxing, ain't it?"

He made a noise of disgust. "Boxing? No!
Boxing's only a side-line with me. I want to be a
boxer, but there's no money in it yet. Katie—I'm
just a common, dirty, side-door burglar—that's what
I am. It was me and a pal what did that business
of cloth from Higginses what's all over the newspapers to-night, and—— Hi! George! Quick—
brandy—quick! Katie's all gone!"

THE HEART OF A CHILD

IV

THE HEART OF A CHILD

A S unsearchable as the heart of kings is the heart of a child. It is good to believe that the heart of a child is the symbol of sunshine, clear as joy; but it is good sometimes to face facts and to recognise that the hearts of children are fashioned in as many shapes and colours as the hearts of men.

In a corner of the saloon bar of the Blue Lantern sat one night Mr. Barney Flowers. Mr. Barney Flowers was a cold, lean man, frugal of speech and comradeship. He kept a small shop in Tonkin Road, in whose outer part he sold newspapers and tobacco. To known applicants at the side-door he sold other things: little packets of powder to put them right after a night at the Lantern, or little packets of powder to put them wrong after a spell of close attention to business. None knew the inner Barney Flowers. He was inaccessible. He sheathed himself, as it were, in a block of ice, and held himself frigid, aloof. As the only man in the district who defied the law by dealing in secret remedies, he was able to do this. All that was known of him was that he kept this shop, and that his home and person were tended by a child, Daisy, assumed to be his daughter, who also delivered the newspapers and served customers with cigarettes. The Blue Lantern saw him at irregular intervals. Then he would come in at opening-time, retire by himself to a corner, and drink until he was stewed.

He was in his usual corner to-night, palpably stewed. He sat with sagging head and damp, drooping mouth, limp fingers precariously supporting an empty glass. Comments passed:

"Barney seems to 'ave 'ad a field day to-day—what?"—"Ar, 'aving 'is reg'lar monthly, eh?"—"Well, 'e's certainly slopped this time. 'E's copped the brewer to-night, fair."

Suddenly, as to the summons of a bell, he seemed to become conscious that his condition was remarked. With shaking hand he deposited the glass on a near table, after trying twice to put it where the table was not. Then he jerked back his head, pulled his lean limbs together, shot himself from his seat, and staggered through the swing doors. As he disappeared, he shot a malevolent glance at the muttering crowd.

"Huh!" said one. "Got 'is monkey up. Now that kid of 'is will 'ave to go through it, I suppose."

He slithered from the bar across the road, down Gill Street, and so to Tonkin Road. He slithered

into his gas-lit shop, mumbling sticky words. His
head rolled from side to side, peering and inquiring.
Seeing nobody, he called in a wet voice, loudly, for
"Dai-see!" None answered him; and after some
seconds of stupid swaying he guided himself to a
stool behind the counter, and sat, fumbling and hiccuping. Some minutes passed.

Then the shop door opened, and a girl entered
with appearance of stealthy panic. A half-smile lit
her face. She moved with a flirt of frock, as one
walking off a stage whereon a conquest has been
made. Her face was the fresh, mobile face of a
child, but at the corners of the mouth knowledge
rested. Her step was peremptory; her manner, for
a child, too self-sufficient. She tossed back her
pouring, dark hair, and smoothed the little frock of
dirty linen. Then she saw the head of Barney
Flowers above the counter; and the smile was shot
away, and the step crawled, and her blood thinned.
She tumbled from challenge to submission.

"Where you bin?" he snapped. Her form
dwindled, and she retreated to the farther wall, like
a gambolling dog suddenly called to order by the
one voice it fears. "Leaving the shop, eh? Slipping
out with them boys again, and leaving everything to
look after itself, and get pinched? Thought I was
out o' the way, and you could pop off? 'Ow many
times 'ave I told you about leaving the shop—eh?
Wodder yeh think yer 'ere for—eh?" He rose from

the stool and steadied himself against the counter.
He pointed with a scraggy arm. "Upstairs. Quick."
He swung round to the door, and glowered; and
slowly she crawled, an abject animal, from the shop
to the narrow stairway.

And suddenly he became sober. He bolted the
shop door, and turned down the lights. From under
the counter he took a clean cane, and passed it
through lean fingers, delicately, as it were a flower.
Then he too moved up the stairs; and soon those in
the Blue Lantern heard, through the jazz music of
voice and glass and beer-engine, and the comment-
ing chit-chat of the cash register, a sharp scream,
followed by a burst of sobs. And they "Tch'd" to
one another, and remarked that Barney was at it
again, and that somebody ought to interfere there,
and look after that kid. But neighbours are shy
of unneighbourly interference. It involves all kinds
of undesirable publicity, and the fierce light that
beats upon the police court witness-box is much too
strong for the sensitive folk of this district. They
shifted the responsibility. "Best thing she can do's
to go to the police, eh?"

Upstairs, in a room empty of furniture, save for
a mattress on the floor, with wall-paper hanging in
dank strips, Barney taught Daisy not to leave the
shop unguarded. The cane in his hands seemed a
living thing, and whistled and sang, and bit and
stung the young, bright body in time with his own

stream of chill profanity. The child, a tumult of frock and raving curls, screamed and writhed, strangling herself with sobs and appeals and efforts to break from the grip that held her down and the flaming thing that leapt about her. Looming above her, Barney whipped her with a kind of dazed ferocity, screaming his words in time with her cries; and the cries rose in pitch until the room seemed filled in every crevice with human wails.

Then, abruptly, the cries and moaning ceased. Barney, with cane held above the disordered figure, paused on the sudden silence. He wrenched her round, and looked close at her, and then stepped back, in dull wonder. She was smiling. Upon her face he saw a curious secret smile that seemed to hang rather under the eyes than about the lips. He had caught her with this smile on the last occasion, and it had disturbed him. He could not understand it. He glared at her now, seeking by a long look to discover its source; and a sudden intense hatred, touched with fear, of her seized him. Then the drink ran back to his brain, and again the rod fell, and again. But now her lips were tight, and she was silent, and nothing was heard in that room but the hiss of the cane and of his breathing.

At last he dropped her, and flung the cane away. His lips were moist and pale. A spot of colour showed on either cheek. His eyes were heavy. As he left her, he looked back for a moment, perplexed.

Then gave it up, and lumbered down the stairs. But the smile haunted him and hurt him and jeered him, and he pondered upon some means whereby he might rid himself of it.

Next morning Daisy went as usual about the house, and at each encounter with Barney she brought to her face that smile, and noted the smile's effect upon him. Barney glowered upon her, and tried to avoid her and her smile; and at last went out to the Blue Lantern to lose it, and found it at the bottom of his glass, and on the floor, and in the air. He drank heavily, and the boys took note of him as he sat in his corner, beating time with a tumbler, and slobbering an old hymn-tune.

At one o'clock Daisy peeked through the swing-door, as though in search of him, and smiled at the company and at him. To the company her smile was a child's smile of salutation, but to Barney it was much more. It was to him a deliberate provocation, a challenge. Like a fool he accepted it. He brandished his glass at her and babbled: "Grr'out! I'll give yeh something to smile at! I'll wipe that smile orf yer face!" and stayed in the bar until half-past two.

At that hour he was put outside, very drunk; so drunk that at the chop suey restaurant, where he customarily took his afternoon meal, he called loudly for a shop steward.

An hour later, at a time when Tonkin Road was filled with people, a high, shrill scream cut cleanly through the gentle stir. Screams of a kind were not uncommon here, but this was no ordinary scream. It was not the pitiful scream of a child being whipped, or the querulous scream of a wife against a violent husband, but the imperative scream of alarm that could not be ignored. And following it came a young, thin voice: " 'Elp! 'Elp! 'E's killing me!"

A constable on a near corner heard it, and, with dignified haste moved to the shop of Mr. Flowers. Encouraged by his presence, the crowd gathered and flowed into the shop behind him and overwhelmed him, and rushed upstairs. In the bare room they saw the child prone on the floor. They saw Barney Flowers dithering over her with infuriated gesture and grimace. They saw him turn, as the leader of the crowd reached the door, and rush upon it to slam it in their faces. But a quick foot and the pressure of many bodies countered the movement, and the room was quickly filled. At this moment the child stirred. Her lips opened, but no sound came. Weakly she raised an arm and pointed it at Barney. Then her arm dropped, and she moved no more.

On the floor at her side lay a tea-cup. The Man Who Knows What To Do, who makes one of every crowd, shouted: "Get that cup! Don't let 'im smash it!" Somebody grabbed the cup. The constable, using valiant elbows, knocked the crowd aside. He went first to the child, made a brief examination, then quietly collared the cup from The Man Who Knew What To Do. He looked into it. He turned to Barney, who stood in the fierce grip of two of the crowd, speechless, white-lipped, damp-faced, glaring. He blew his whistle and hustled the crowd away.

Well, of course Barney was arrested and, later, hanged. At the trial local witnesses, eager now to come forward when the affair had assumed wide importance, showed, to the satisfaction of the twelve good tradesmen in the box, that the child had gone in terror of Barney; that he had consistently ill-treated and threatened her; that she was not his child, but had been bought by him from a tramp woman; that he kept stocks of poison in which he did illicit business; that nobody was in the house that afternoon save himself and the child; that the dregs of the poison found in the tea-cup corresponded to poison of which he held a supply, and that a new packet of it had been opened that day; that the child was insured for twenty pounds; and that he was a man of vicious turn of mind to whom the taking of life weighed little against his own dreadful inclinations. Then there was the child's last cry for help, heard by ten witnesses, and her last gesture of accusation, to which there were six witnesses.

His demeanour in the dock greatly assisted the case for the prosecution. He protested his innocence furiously, with fevered movements, inarticulately, with torrents of words and sudden dams of speechlessness. He contradicted himself clumsily many times. But his whirling explanations were beaten down by the evidence.

So they hanged him. You see, the general knowledge of the child mind is so slender that while men will credit the darkest and most tortuous motives to the adult mind, they are ever sure that a child could never carry out, or even conceive, the simplest scheme of spite or retribution. Not one member of the coroner's jury thought twice about the smile which Daisy wore in death—a chill, clear smile of triumphant satisfaction.

THE DUMB WIFE

V

THE DUMB WIFE

DARK is this tale of love with woe as dark as the malefic arches that shut out light from the streets about the water-side. In these streets it is always chilly afternoon, grey-hued and empty of happy noise and welcoming windows. Here the narrow kerbs make boundaries for the puckered lives of their people; and feet fall without echo upon their stones.

Yet, though all else perish here, beauty and love and sacrifice survive. In these waste places below London river mean iniquities propagate and flourish, and curl their soiling arms about all that would be brave and beautiful. Yet beauty persists. Even in the heart of darkness love takes root and spreads therein its eternal enchantments of gardens and moonrise and April airs and song.

In one of these infelicitous streets, some distance from the main Chinese quarter, stood a small Chinese laundry. At an upper window of this laundry sat, for many years, a woman of semi-Oriental features. Day by day, month by month, she sat there, the object of that pity which those deep in misfortune bestow so largely upon others in misfortune. Part of her story was known. She was the wife of the owner of the laundry, Ng Yong; and she was dumb.

Throughout the hours of light she sat at her window, her naturally placid face now coldly blank by her affliction; staring at nothing, hearing nothing; silent and still; a piece of Chinese carving. And deep in her narrow eyes lay a crouching horror, so that strangers, passing that window, quickened their steps to the friendly main road. What passed each day behind that rigid face may not be known; can only be conjectured. What hate—what fear—what resolution of vengeance and escape—what vacillation—what dark ideas and darker memories gathered there—these things are not to be told.

Upon recurring occasions she would, without warning, shed her impassivity, and a scene would follow. She would run to the door and strive for speech to the point of paroxysm, and utter anomalous noises, and make wild gestures in the direction of West India Dock. Then her husband would hasten to her. He would take her in hand, sadly, and lead her, with kind firmness, back to seclusion; and the neighbours would murmur in sympathy with him and his forbearance under his trials.

He had early explained to them the misfortune that had befallen his house, and they had often aided him in quieting the sufferer. On her rare walks he went always with her, the ministering husband; when she turned and turned from street to street, as though in search of one desired spot, and stopped passers-by with her pleading face and working jaws, he would make forlorn play with his hands, and strangers would draw away, and those who knew would gather about him.

This much was known. Here is the full story.

When Moy Toon was born in Poplar of an English mother and a Chinese father there was no warm place for her with her father's people, and none at all with her mother's. Her father's people, however, finding her lying about unclaimed, and holding something of grace within them, did provide her with bare necessaries. Left motherless in her early years, she was received into a tea-house in the colony to do the rough work. In this tea-house she spent many tedious years whose days she scarcely counted. She had little capacity for thought; felt little; asked little; was as content as the slave born in slavery and untaught. Her birth had given her a larger share of Oriental compliance than of Western scepticism and challenge. Things were what they were, and she accepted them. She grew up in the promiscuous company of the docks. Of moral training she had little, and no learning beyond that given of custom to the Chinese woman of the coolie class. So she passed her young years in a kind of somnambulism.

Then one night there came to the tea-house, in the fourth stage of inebriety, a young second mate. She had seen him many times about the streets; and, in her aimless way, had admired his happy stride and clear, sea-brightened face. On this occasion the wavering charm of the girl, unsettled between English mobility and Eastern gravity, captivated his beer-bound senses, and he made proposals to her. He had but to invite, and she went, her warped spirit mildly pleased at the attention from this man-wonder.

Well, that night was the first of many. He made a fuss of her, and called her Baby Doll and other babbling names, and bought cheap gifts for her. On his next time ashore he again sought her out, and pleased himself with her simple company. Some months later he made a definite parting from her, telling her only that he was about to marry and settle down in another part of London; and she saw him no more. She took her dismissal placidly, without rancour, as she took all things, whether blows or endearments, and asked nothing of him.

Later came the baby. The restaurant-keeper was a little chagrined at this clumsy misdemeanour, but he gave her rough attention, and the child was placed with an old woman, known to the Chinese

colony, who lived at Blackwall. Now Moy Toon
became quite silly about that baby. It was her
living memory of the one adventure of her life,
and she worshipped it. At first she clung to it
defiantly, as a gesture of disdain against those about
her who so lightly esteemed her wonderful achieve-
ment of motherhood. But in a more sober moment
she saw that in their advice lay her best course.
With the child, she could not hope to earn even
the scanty living that her abilities and known story
permitted her to command to-day; and she had no
taste for the life which other girls of her birth
and class affected. She had had her one adventure, and desired, for the child's sake, to walk
securely. She preferred the rough comfort of the
tea-house to the dolorous enterprise of the streets.
She knew that the child would receive, under
other protection, at least the essentials of life,
which she herself could not faithfully promise him.
So she let wisdom beat down her sentiment, and
surrendered the child, with the condition that she
should see it from time to time as she wished.

For six years, then, she followed her arid course,
mother and no mother, accepting, without question or conjecture, the untowardness of her circum-
stance; rather giving thanks that her course was
broken, week by week, by visits to the boy. Often
during these years her pillow shook to the vibra-
tions of her sobbing breast, as she recalled the

young strength and delicate small ways of him, and reached vain arms through the darkness to the child she might not openly claim. In the rough-and-tumble of the dock-side alleys he had grown into a wiry, alert urchin, big and bold for his age; and delicious afternoons she spent with him, dressing him in a travesty of seaman's uniform—reefer jacket and gilt buttons, with peaked cap and much cheap braid about it—and calling him "Mother's Sailor Boy"; afternoons that compensated for the lonely nights.

Then old Ng Yong appeared. He had bought the laundry business of a compatriot who was returning to his own country, and he was doing very well with it. But, looking round the fittings of the house, which he had bought with the business, he felt that something was lacking, and discovered that it lacked a woman. He felt that a woman would be an agreeable piece of furniture, and would finish off the establishment. He looked about for one, and at the tea-house of the Hundred Gilded Dragons he found Moy Toon. Moy Toon seemed to him to be just the article. He inquired of the keeper of the house concerning her, and found that she was available, and was in the gift of the keeper.

Now Ng Yong was very strict on the sanctity of womanhood (from the prospective purchaser's point of view) and put to the keeper voluminous questions upon her life and behaviour. These the

man behind the Gilded Dragons answered freely:
not entirely truthfully, but freely, with an engaging
air of candour. When Ng Yong demanded assur-
ances of the unblemished character of the goods,
these also he freely gave. No gentleman of com-
merce has yet been known to cry down his wares;
and he knew that the disclosure of a certain adventure would appreciably lower the price of the article
to that of shop-soiled.

Moy Toon was privately told of the opening of
negotiations, and was shown, by reports of Ng
Yong's prosperity, how largely her situation should
be uplifted by an alliance with him, and how necessary it was that the existence of the boy should
be kept secret. It was urged upon her that she
should renounce for ever any further part in him;
but to that she answered nothing. To the pro-
posed union she offered no objection. Ng Yong
was old, but she was not repelled on that ground:
she was sufficiently Chinese to regard the difference
in ages as fitting. She saw here a chance of helping
herself, and, indirectly, the boy, and was prepared
to take it without a second thought. She never
doubted her ability to keep her own secret.

So, some nights later, she was inspected and
questioned by Ng Yong, who expressed himself as
satisfied with her person and with her demeanour
of modesty. But he did not let the serious occasion
of wife-taking pass without administering a sharp

lecture on wifely deportment. He sat before her
in the kitchen of the tea-house, his fleshy hands
splayed upon his knees, his old head wagging, the
secrets of his eyes shaded from the groping minds
of his fellows. Ng Yong's wife, he told her, must be
obedient; must give unquestioning and unceasing
service to her lord; must give ready and regular
attention to household duties; must sever all con-
nection with the people about the tea-house; and,
above all, must be honest and faithful. She must
be all his and his alone. He quoted passages from
the Four Books concerning the Virtuous Wife, and
the others; and his voice dropped to a muttered
monotone as he spoke of the punishment befitting
the wife who failed in the first law.

To this homily Moy Toon listened prefunctorily,
and answered casually, with modest and low-toned
responses. So the business proceeded, through many
evenings of bargaining, until at last a middle price
was agreed, the money paid to the Gilded Dragons,
and Moy Toon lifted over the threshold of Ng
Yong.

All that he required of her in service and obedience she gave him. But she would not renounce
her boy. Her heart had not been asked of her,
and that she kept; and in it, guarded from all profane contact, rested the boy. He was her joss, and
through him and before him she worshipped. For
the rest, she served Ng Yong well. She had no

desire to do else. She was scrupulous in anticipating his wishes, studious in attending the house, and looked at no other man.

Of this she had but little chance, for her husband was ever about her. Maybe her demeanour of modesty had not wholly convinced him. He watched her with vigilant eyes; never was she free from him; and even when she was out on shopping business she felt that she was under his regard.

Her meetings with her boy became, therefore, matters of delicacy. To go to the house in Canning Town, each Thursday, as she had done these six years, would at once arouse suspicion. He would note these regular, recurring disappearances; he would question her and perhaps not be satisfied by her answers; he would follow her or have her followed, and discover her secret; and then the pavement would receive her, and she and the boy would starve.

She considered carefully new arrangements, and decided that future meetings must be haphazard, snatched at odd moments, and a different rendezvous must be appointed for each meeting. Discretion warned her to follow the Dragon's advice and abandon wholly these meetings. She was safe now and comfortable, and her daily life was well set. Better to take the chance of seeing the boy at a distance, without speech, or of getting word of his welfare from independent parties, than to risk all her present security and well-being for the idle whim of fondling him and talking with him. For discovery meant banishment from the house of Ng Yong and consequent privation and misery. Beyond that her mind did not travel. Of the words of his homily on wifely decorum she remembered nothing: they had gone, as the phrase is, in at one ear and out at the other. He would be angry and kick her out, and she and the boy would suffer. And suffering of any kind she could not face. She hated it and feared it.

Yet, upon a night in the first month of marriage, as she lay awake, she thought of the boy and fancied his small arms about her, and his voice whispering childish prayers for pennies in her ear. Her boy. Next morning she managed to pass the word, through many channels, to the woman who had charge of him, that she should bring him, the following afternoon, to Tunnel Gardens. There she could sit with him and the woman, and hear him talk; and if Ng Yong or any friend of his should see her thus engaged, she could reply, quite suitably, that the woman and the boy were strangers; that the child at play had attracted her and she had spoken to him and his mother. No harm in that. So it was done, without misadventure.

For the next meeting, a fortnight later, she appointed a sweetstuff shop near Blackwall, where the boy was fed with cakes and ginger-beer. She

spent an hour with him here, and when she returned, Ng Yong, who was customarily superin-
tending the laundry at that hour, was awaiting her
upstairs. He told her that she had been long gone;
and she answered that she had gone to the cheaper
market at Shadwell, and had been delayed because
the road was under repair. He looked strangely
and closely at her, but she caught nothing of the
look. Her eyes were full of her boy—how bonny
he was looking and how pert of manner.

The next meeting she fixed, after some thought,
for a morning in a disused cellar in a remote corner
near West India Dock. She had discovered this cellar some years ago, and it was to-day much as it
was then. She and her sailor had spent some hours
there one wet evening of summer, when he had
been unable to find other temporary accommodation. It was easily entered, and, as it held nothing
that could be stolen, was never under observation.
It had lain abandoned since the river first entered
it and swamped its contents. Repairs had been attempted, but the river persisted; and at every high
tide it was waist-deep in water. It was entered from
a narrow passage by a flight of broken steps so
hidden that none could without guidance discover
them.

Hither, then, the boy was brought. The cellar,
lit by Moy Toon's electric torch, did not daunt him.
He was a lad of his father's spirit, she told herself,

for he was delighted with the adventure, and
trotted about the place, prying here and there, and
nourishing his mother's heart with smiles. She
stood by him, blooming with pride and encouraging
his tricks, careless of all save the small circle in
which he moved. But in the midst of his gambolling
the woman who had brought him lifted a nervous
finger.

"Listen! Quiet!"

He stopped suddenly, and Moy Toon gathered
him against her skirt. They listened.

"Oo—er!" croaked the woman. "Someone
comin'. I was afraid we'd get into trouble comin'
'ere. What'll we do? Where shall we go? Oo—
er. I'm gointer get outer this. It's your affair. I
ain't in it. I ain't gointer be mixed up in no———"

With a whirl of worried skirts and cumbrous
boots, she pounded up the steps. Moy Toon, below,
heard a sound as of a dull impact, and a shrill "Oo—
er!" followed by "Look out, gel!"

It was a moment of panic. The woman had seen
something to affright her, and Moy Toon's first instinct was the boy. At that moment she was without power of thought. She saw three feet from
her an alcove in which the boy had been exploring.
It was guarded by a heavy door with a great iron
hasp and lock. She grabbed the boy by the arm,
and put her mouth to his ear.

"In there, darling. Quick—in there. Don't make
a sound. It's for mummy."

The boy understood and hopped into the alcove.
She swept the door upon him and snapped it close.
She turned from it to reach the torch and extinguish
it; and turned to see Ng Yong descending the last
step to the cellar, with hand outstretched in command which she instinctively obeyed. He reached
the bottom, and stood motionless, looking about
him, right and left. The sudden shock of his arrival,
and the closing of the door, had left her breathless,
incapable of act or word. She leaned against the
wall, panting, her slow mind rolling round one idea:
"What did he see? What did he see?" Through
his silence she prayed for him to speak.

At last he spoke, quietly: "So this is where you
meet your lover? Let us see him."

"Lover? Me? No, I don't. Oh no—no—I
don't. What d'you mean?"

She knew that she was speaking stupidly, uncon-
vincingly, but delight at his mistake about a lover
made her careless. Inside herself she laughed. If
she had to suffer his wrath, she would suffer; but
at least the boy was safe, while the lover idea
remained.

"Where is your lover?"

"Lover? I ain't got no lover."

"What then would you be doing here?"

"But—I mean—there ain't no lover. I come 'ere to——"

"So you come to this place—this place—to gossip with old women, huh? Bring out your lover."

"But I ain't——" She saw suddenly that her best plan, for the boy's sake, was to hold the idea of a lover, to develop it.

"Well, I mean, suppose I——"

He raised a hand. "Look at me!"

The instinct of obedience raised her eyes, and she looked full at him, and what she saw in his face turned her sick. She gibbered.

"But I ain't—I ain't——"

"You—you to whom I gave my trust. Oh, child of a dog!"

"But I mean—I——"

A snarl broke from his lips. His hand dipped to his inner pocket. She watched it with foolish eyes, fumbling under his canvas coat. She saw it come out, holding a long curved knife, the blade dulled by long disuse. He held it by the ivory hilt, directed the point upon her, horizontally, and slowly, quietly approached her. Like dropping water, the words of his homily on the Virtuous Wife dropped through her mind.

"You have chosen your place well. We are safe here. I told you how I would punish unfaithfulness."

With each step forward he took, she took one

backward, shrinking from him. He followed her.
She drew back, shuddering, arms extended, pressing
herself against the wall as if she would force herself into it. He followed her. Pat-pat, pat-pat,
they moved softly along the damp floor. She continued to step slow paces backward, eyes fixed on
him. He followed her. He followed her until she
had reached the far wall, where an iron grating
gave out to the river. There she stood, mouthing
at him, cornered; fascinated, rabbit-like, by the dull
tongue of steel that slowly floated towards her
breast. Nearer and nearer it came. She felt the
touch of it upon her corsage; then the prick of it
upon her skin; and at this she opened wide her
throat to scream: "Mercy! Mercy! I ain't got
no lover!"

But, though she opened her throat, none of
these words came. Her mouth opened and shut,
and her teeth came together and flew apart; but
no sound could she utter. The knife rose and
fluttered half-an-inch from her throat. Then Ng
Yong dropped it to his waist, and drew back. He
looked long at her before he spoke again.

"Where is this lover?"

Her lips moved, and she made meaningless noises,
and shook her head and prayed with her hands.
Ng Yong replaced the knife in his coat, and nodded
gravely. The shock of discovery and the threatened
punishment had taken punishment from his hands.

His wife was punished by an instrument keener than any blade of steel. She was struck dumb.

He took her by the arm. She shuddered at the touch, and he smiled upon her. He drew her to the steps leading to the alley. As he led her away, she struggled, and pointed to the great door of the alcove, and made low noises: "Myw! Myw!"

Ng Yong, too, looked at the door, and gave a smile of understanding. With easy force he compelled her up the steps. She beat against his bent arm, and strove with hands and lips, as one explaining. But he led her away, quietly, down that narrow passage, so that none noted their going until they reached the main road. And he led her home, and told sympathetic inquirers how his wife had suffered a sad shock from a street accident, which had deprived her of speech and made her foolish of mind.

BLUEBELL

— VI —

BLUEBELL

SLIPPERY SAM, the copper's nark, stood in the bar of the Blue Lantern and drank bitter, while he complained to his only friend, Hank Hogan, the odd messenger, of the present discontents. At the other end of the bar a group of the Roseleaf Boys, who "worked" the West End shopping crowds, delivered to the world generally, in high voices, their opinions of Slippery Sam.

"Thinks 'isself smart, y'know. I reckon we got a beat on 'im lars' week." "Smart! Huh! Nosing round Chinatown for dope shops is about all 'e's fit for." "Planted the bunce right under 'is dirty nose, I did." "Why, take a dekko at 'im. 'E looks like 'is job. Any side-door cadger'd know it first time. Goes about with a black mask on and a brass band in front of 'im, playing 'I'm the copper's nark.'" "Yerce, if a faro crib opened next door to 'im and 'ung out signs, 'e wouldn't know it for a week or two."

Here the voices dropped. Slippery Sam had not heard what was spoken loudly, but he heard what

was murmured; his ears were adjusted that way.
"Yerce, old 'Awkins 'as started a shop in Cable
Street. Bin running these four weeks. *'E* dunno
it, though. 'E'll 'ear about it like 'e 'ears everything else—when 'e reads it in the papers."

Slippery Sam drank up, excused himself to his
friend and went out.

The boys were right. He hadn't heard about it.
But the name caught his ear, and he thought of
a gentle walk to Cable Street. On another point
the boys were wrong. He was good for something
besides nosing for dope shops in Chinatown. He
was good for nosing round women. He nosed
round them like a dog. He sniffed. He fawned.
He snapped. He snarled. He patted and mauled
and showed his teeth. He was nosing round one
now. Bluebell Hawkins. But in her case he
could not snarl or show his teeth. There was nothing to bite on. Or there had been nothing to
bite on. But the information given to him by
the sour temper of the Roseleaf Boys indicated
something substantial. Old Hawkins had started
a Shop. In Shadwell a Shop means one thing. It
does not mean a gambling den or a dancing den
or a coining den or a shebeen; it means a Shop.

As he passed up Gravel Lane there was a sudden
outcry of young voices:

"Come on, boys! 'Ere's Sing-a-song Joe!
Chase 'im, boys! Muck 'im about!"

Slippery Sam stopped to watch and chuckle.
Against a wall crouched a lanky, thin-faced, wispy-
haired youth, in tatterdemalion clothes. In his lean
fingers he held a tin whistle. With this and with
lifted leg he made aimless, slow gestures of defense,
while his face wore the silly smile of the victim who
tries to enter into the joke of his persecution. His
mouth made childish noises of protest. Slippery
Sam stood by and grinned. This was Sing-a-song
Joe, the half-witted character of the district; sometimes drunk, sometimes running amok; but always
the butt of the street boys, and always stupidly
cheerful. When things were dull and amusement
wanting, there was always Sing-a-song Joe to be
dug out and baited. Whence he came none knew.
He had appeared among them as a lad in knicker-
bockers. The Union would not have him; the
Asylum would not have him; the police were bored
with him. He was helpless and harmless. His
bed was any archway sheltered from the breeze.
His food he cadged by promises—or, as some said,
threats—to sing a song in return for broken scraps
or cigarettes or beer. From those who knew him
he mostly got the gift, and was hastily released from
his promise of entertainment. It was only when
he approached a stranger that the price would be
accepted and the neighbourhood disturbed by frightful discords on his whistle, or additional horror

lent by his cracked voice to obscene soldier and sailor songs.

Slippery Sam stood and watched and urged on the boys. Then suddenly, through the crowd, broke the slim, bright figure of a young girl. She cuffed right and left with her hands, and came to the side of Sing-a-song, striking with words.

"Let 'im alone, yeh little beasts. You leave 'im be. Never mind, Sing-a-song, I'll see to 'em. Here, mike off quick. Little blackguards, can't yeh leave the boy alone?"

With profane comment and derisive gestures the boys strolled away to the next amusement, and she put an arm about the victim.

"They bin hustling you, Sing-a-song?" she asked gently.

He giggled. "No, no. I don't mind. They alwis do it. They like a bit o' fun. They think I'm cracked. But *you* know, don't yeh? You know I'm all right? I like you, Bluebell. You're kind to me."

She smiled upon him. "You ought to stick up for yourself, boy, you're big enough now. Hit 'em. Knock 'em about. I know there's a crowd of 'em, but you hit one, hard, and it'll frighten the others. See?"

"Oh, no, Bluebell, that ain't right. They don' mean nothing. Wouldn't be right to 'urt 'em."

Slippery Sam strolled up. " 'Ullo, missie."

Bluebell Hawkins looked round and shuddered sharply. She moved closer to the half-witted Sing-a-song.

"Hullo."

Sing-a-song observed that she was engaged. "I'll go, Bluebell," he piped, humbly withdrawing.

Bluebell stretched a hand. "No, don't." But, putting his whistle to his lips, and blowing a piercing blast, he capered round the corner and away.

"Seem fond o' Sing-a-song," remarked Slippery conversationally.

"Oh?"

"Yerce. Never take no notice of yer friends when they pass in the streets, but always looking after 'im."

Bluebell thought of a rude retort, but did not make it. She was not sure of Slippery. She loathed him. The fact of his being in her neighbourhood affected her as the presence of a cat affects some people. And, somehow, though she felt no fear, she had a notion that he was to be feared.

"What if I do?" she said. "He wants some-one to look after him, when everybody's tormenting him. Why should they? He's only a bit soft. There's nothing nasty or wicked about him. That boy'd do anything in the world for me."

"Well, perhaps 'e would. Perhaps other people would, too. What could 'e do for yeh, though? 'E's no good to anyone. Can't even look after 'isself. There's other people that might be yer friends—real friends—and do things for yeh, if yeh'd let 'em. Nobody never knows when they might want a friend—a real friend."

He looked at her and his eyes raked her face and then—or so she felt—raked off her clothes and grinned upon her young body. She shuddered again and moved beyond him. His sloppy clothes, his sloppy limbs, his sloppy movements nauseated her. There was an odour of slops all about him. "Well, I must be going."

"Right-o. But don't forget what I said. A friend's a friend. And yeh never know."

She walked swiftly from him, in some trouble at his words. She walked lightly, and her feet barely disturbed the dust of the pavement. In Juniper Street, where was her home, she was known as That Refined Girl. It was agreed that she was Quite The Lady. There was gentleness in every line of her. Even the massed yellow of her hair seemed gentle against the brutal bricks and girders and the insistent dun of Shadwell; and the startling combination of light curls with deep brown eyes lent her an air of waywardness that caused remark in a place where all things were blunt and deter-mined. Her merry hat, her bright mouth, her swinging arms gave a moment's courage to the cringing street as she passed; but her heart was troubled.

Mr. Hawkins, her father, had long done well in the second-hand wardrobe business; but lately he had disposed of his stock and goodwill, and was now much at home. He had told Bluebell, in a casual way, that he had started another business, in a new line, but what that business was she was not told. Certainly, it seemed more profitable than second-hand clothes, for there was more money about the house. He did himself well, and gave Bluebell presents of new hats and frocks, and added many necessary comforts to their home. But Bluebell had wondered about this business, and his evasion of her questions. Lately, nasty words had crept about the district, and had been borne, by the sluggish wind of gossips' breath, to her ears. She began to scrutinise her father at the supper-table, while he was engaged with the evening paper; and, at last, putting words together, she framed something like the truth. She confirmed it by questions to Sing-a-song Joe, who heard everything; and he told her, innocently, not knowing whether the business was good or bad, its nature.

She had not known it long before her father discovered that she knew. Without a word from either, mutual knowledge was discovered; and thereafter the bright tones of the Hawkins' home was subdued. Though never proclaimed, the knowledge pervaded the house like a fog. This nasty grey Fact loomed over them, and sat between them at the fireside, and hovered above the table as they sat at meals, and sucked the warmth from their words and their advances, and lent a chill to any attempt at candid intercourse. And there were dreadful occasions when Hawkins would say, in the tones of a clumsy actor who has memorised a part till it becomes meaningless: "Well, girl, I shall be rather late to-night. Special business to see to, y'know. Don't wait up for me." And Bluebell would reply in the same tones: "All right, dad; I'll leave something cold on the table for you."

She did not dare to name to him her knowledge and her horror. Though a strong, undemonstrative love united them, his dark temper ·had always forbidden any attempt on her part to challenge any attitude or action on his. Don't think that she suffered any pangs of conscience at enjoying the new good things provided by this more prosperous business. She didn't. Nor, perhaps, was she at all concerned with the "wrong" side of it. It was to her only a thoroughly nasty business. What horrified and disgusted her, savagely insistent as she was on chastity, and loathing the fact of sex, was the dirtiness, the animalism, the disgrace of it.

He was not often out late. He was out at odd times morning and evening, but usually returned at ten o'clock. The place of business in Cable Street Bluebell had discovered. There he went each morning to collect the money paid by the night's visitors, and to see that order was maintained among the terrible company who called themselves face-tiously his "staff." He was always quietly dressed; sleek; reticent in style and speech. A black beard lent him circumspection, and his manner was like a dark alley of shuttered houses. He was always, to his neighbours, "Mr." Hawkins.

As Bluebell prepared the table for supper to-night the words of Slippery Sam still clattered in her head; and when at his proper hour her father came in, she quizzed him. He sat at the table with the evening paper, not, as usual, tranquil and self-contained. He fidgeted. Bluebell observed. After eating, he spoke.

"You know Sam Booth?"

"What—him they call Slippery Sam?"

" 'M."

"Yes, everybody does." The tone of voice clearly conveyed "and loathes him."

"Oh, well—not a bad chap. I rather like him. You don't seem to?"

"Well, can you ask? Like him? How can one like a rat or a snake or anything slimy?"

"Oh, he's not as bad as all that. You mustn't believe all people say about him. He's not really such a bad chap. However, I·only asked. But you might be a bit nice to him. I saw him this evening, and he seemed to think you wanted to be rude to

him. Be a bit nice, like. Because—y'see—I mean
—he might be able to do me a good turn."

Bluebell knew what her father was trying to say,
and he knew that she knew; and her breasts seemed
suddenly two blocks of ice. But she only answered:
"Oh, well, you'd have to be pretty hard up to take
favours from a worm like that." And she served
him with beer, and they spoke no more until "Good-
night."

Next morning when she went shopping Slippery
Sam stepped from an alley into her path, and simu-
lated surprise. " 'Ullo, Bluebell. Out early, eh?
My word, what a nobby frock! That cost a bit, I
lay. But it ain't too good for you, whatever it
cost. Your dad's doing well just now, eh?"

She moved to pass him. "I believe so. . . .
Well, I got a lot of things to get this morning."

" 'Arf a mo'. I got something serious to say
to you. I mean it, reely. Something that concerns
you. Supposing your dad was in trouble, and you
could 'elp 'im. Would yeh?"

"Don't be silly. You know me an' dad would
do anything for one another."

She looked steadily at him and he at her. He
wondered if she knew; but her face was the face
of a pretty girl busy with domestic matters.

"Well, I won't keep yeh now. I'll tell yeh later.
I don't want to worry your little 'ead. I dessay yer

father's told yeh already that he might be in trouble some time."

Bluebell walked on shuddering; partly from contact with Slippery, and partly from his words. She brooded and fretted all day, and that night her father spoke his awful lines: "Well, girl, I shall be rather late to-night. Special business to see to, y'know. Don't wait up for me." To which she made the customary reply.

Half-an-hour after he was gone came a knock at the street door. She opened it and found Slippery Sam.

"Want to come in," he said hoarsely. "Want to talk to yeh, private-like."

Her arm ached to slam the door upon his nose, but something restrained her. She let him enter. He slouched into the kitchen and stood awkwardly by the table.

"It's true what I told yeh 'smorning," he began. "I found out about it. There'll be trouble fer you and your dad before long. But it *could* be stopped. I could get it stopped, I think."

She looked at him with orderly eyes. "Well, suppose it is true? What about it? Why come and tell me?"

"Well, yeh said 'smorning yeh'd do anything to 'elp your dad if 'e was in trouble. Well, now yeh got a chance, so I thought I'd tell yeh."

"I see. You want to be squared, I suppose. How much do you want?"

"Ah, I see you've rumbled it. But—er—well, it ain't a matter o' money. I can get money easy. There's some things better'n money. I thought I'd come to-night, seeing yer dad go out; 'cos if 'e 'eard you was ready to save 'im this way, very likely 'e wouldn't let yeh. Might be ready to stand the racket 'isself, rather'n you should be—er—bothered. But I reckon you wouldn't like to let 'im in fer—well— bad trouble, when you could easy prevent it."

She rested a hand on the kitchen table and leant across it.

"What is it you want, you—beast?"

Then he smiled and his awkwardness dropped from him. This was a language he understood. He asserted himself.

"Why, if yeh look in the glass, ducky, yeh don't need to ask a man that. You know what I want."

She took a deep breath, as though to blow him from the room. Then she recovered and spoke quietly. "No, you slimy reptile. No. Get out— quick!"

He did not move. "Nice words from *you*—slimy reptile—from *you*. And who are *you?* Where did that pretty frock come from? Where did those shoes come from? Eh? Who's worse—you, that swank about in new 'ats and frocks and look the lady, or the poor gels what make the money that buys 'em? Eh? D'yeh know what your father is? 'E's a——"

She clapped hands to ears. "Don't say it. Beast. Don't say it. Oh!"

"Ar! I see yeh know. And still try to be the lady. Well, it won't last long, y'know. Not only your being a lady won't last. There's worse. Your dad'll be taken to the court. 'E'll be committed for trial. It'll all be printed in the papers. Twelve munce is a light sentence for that. An' 'e'll be put in convick dress, and be 'eating 'is 'eart out in a cell, and working at miserable work—and not a soul to talk to all the time. 'E'll be thinking of you— every minute of the day and 'arf the night. And where'll you be? Eh? When it's all exposed— where'll you be? 'Ere? No. You'll be chased out of the place. You won't 'ave nowhere to go. You won't—you won't 'ave a place to lay yer 'ead. No- body'll look at yeh, when they know. Yeh'll be where the girls are what bring the money fer yer pretty frocks and 'ats. That's where *you'll* be, unless—— 'Arf-a-dozen words from me and—flip- flop!"

She dropped into a chair and hid her face. "Don't, don't! You beast! Oh, go away."

He approached her. "Now don't be silly, gel. I'll give y'a chance. Gimme a kiss now, and I won't do nothing for a day or two. I'll let yeh think it over. Come on."

He shook her shoulder. She writhed at the touch, but she thought of father in prison, and slowly she rose, her lips parted in misery and disgust. Her skin tingled. He stood motionless at her side.

"Come on, gel."

Slowly she put her face to his, and gave him her bright mouth. He grabbed her neck and pressed his tight lips hard against hers, and she sobbed and her throat made noises of revolt. "There! That's that! I'll go now, and you be sensible and think it over."

She sank to the table again, and when she looked up he was gone.

Long she sat thus, staring before her, while grim, grey thoughts moved nakedly across her mind. Then, chilled with solitude, she got up, took hat and coat, and went out. She did not know and did not care where she would walk—she wanted to be out. Suddenly, as she passed a lampless alley, the quiet of the street was rent by a screaming note from a tin whistle, and she knew that Sing-a-song Joe was about. She followed the direction of the sound, for she felt that Sing-a-song was the one person she could meet to-night. With Sing-a-song she could and did talk freely. She could tell him things she dare not tell to others—little fancies, whims, desires, that would have aroused bitter ridicule in others. He was a child. She could unpack her

mind to him in speech,without fear of compromising
herself by revelation.

She found him strutting gaily over the cobbles,
whistle at mouth. He stopped at sight of her, and,
though the inane smile remained on his face, his
voice conveyed concern.

"'Ullo, Bluebell. Don't yeh feel well, Bluebell?
You got a pain anywhere, Bluebell?"

"Oh, Sing-a-song, I'm so unhappy. I'm in trouble,
Sing-a-song."

"What? Ain't you had your dinner, Bluebell!
Or you lost your purse—or what?"

"No, it isn't anything like that, Sing-a-song.
Here, come down here."

"That's right, Bluebell. You tell Sing-a-song all
about it. You alwis look after Sing-a-song, so 'e'll
look after you."

Up and down the side street they walked for
half-an-hour, while Bluebell told him, in plain, set
terms that he could understand, the nature of her
trouble. She did not tell him with any idea of finding advice or assistance, but because she must discharge her mind of its burden of horror, and he
was the one person to whom she could confess
without surrender of dignity and esteem. Cackles
of thin laughter, which from Sing-a-song meant sympathy, interspersed her monotonous recital; and
when he heard that Slippery Sam was the occasion
of her troubled eyes and lagging steps, he shuffled

his feet and blew wild notes on his whistle. Slippery Sam was his enemy too, and never failed to give himself cheap sport by setting the street urchins about the witless boy when he found him.

"Oh, Bluebell," he bleated. "Poor Bluebell! Never mind; don't you cry. And don't you be afraid of Slippery Sam. Poor Bluebell!"

That was all the comfort he could give her. But when he left her, and shuffled towards the Great Eastern arches to bed, blowing weird music from his whistle, his thoughts ran upon the business. His beautiful lady, his princess, was in trouble, and had told him all about it. But what could a softy do? Nobody would take any notice of him. Softy, they would call him. He wondered if he could kill Slippery Sam. It would be nice if he could. Bluebell would admire him for that. But Slippery Sam was a strong man and could fight. Then people would find out that he had been killed, and there was awful punishment for that kind of thing. At this point a lantern flashed upon him, as he crouched under the arch. He sprang nimbly to his feet, but a voice reassured him. It was the voice of P. C. Gossett, the only constable in that district who never annoyed or hustled him. He liked P. C. Gossett. He was a good policeman and big and strong and calm.

"All right, kid," said Gossett. "I didn't know it was you. Settle down and be good."

"Slippery Sam's a bad man," said Sing-a-song in-consequently.

"Just found that out, boy? Most people knew that a long time ago."

"Sing-a-song don't like Slippery Sam. 'E's unkind to people."

"No more don't I, old man. We ain't loved one another for a long time. But don't you worry. One o' these days I'll get him, and then he won't give you nor nobody else any trouble. I'm only waiting fer me chance. Now be'ave yesself, boy, and I'll see yer not shifted from here. Here—here's a crust of bread and cheese—bit o' my supper, but I don't fancy cheese to-night."

Sing-a-song grabbed the food and ate it; and all through the night he lay awake on the stones. The morning gave him an idea. One way there was, he saw suddenly, by which his Bluebell might be saved: a drastic way, which might put some pain upon her, but a pain less hideous and enduring than that which now threatened her. It was the only way he could see to assuage her present misery; and he set himself to take it.

For a week of evenings the atmosphere of the Hawkins' home was like a dark forest, where surly red fire smouldered. The great Fact that sat always between them at table had now a shadowy companion—a grim Idea that crouched behind it and made terrible grimaces at Bluebell. Darker and darker grew her father's manner, retreating from her day by day, until it seemed that never again would they reach one another; and day by day she suffered double torture: the torture of his strained face and the torture of Slippery Sam with his "Well, gel, when am I goin' to 'ave more'n a kiss, eh?" until she felt each night that the breaking-point had been reached, and the torture must be ended by the one act of sacrifice that was demanded.

At the end of the week the surly red broke into fierce flame. Hawkins came home early that evening, before ten o'clock. He dropped heavily into the chair by the kitchen stove. Bluebell brought a bottle of beer and poured him a glass. She placed it on the table at his elbow, but he did not drink. He looked deep into the fire, and spoke slowly:

"Er—Bluebell—girl."

"'M?"

"Got some bad news for you?"

"Bad news? Oh—bad news. Yes, what now? Bad news?"

She was standing at the cupboard, replacing the bottle. He saw only her back. It was bent as to receive a blow.

"Yerce. I'm in trouble."

"Trouble?" The voice was a shred of a voice, naked. "You in trouble? And——Oh, go on."

He turned round in the chair, faced her and spoke quickly, without a pause between phrases.

"Yes, girl, trouble. Big trouble. I'm going to be—I mean the police are after me. I bin doing wrong—running a crook business, and I'm going to be locked up. I can't get away. They know who I am and where I live, and they'll be here any minute now. I bin running a bad house, and somebody's give me away."

The bottle slipped from her hand and fell with a jagged crash to the floor. She turned and faced him; and even in his own deep misery he thought he had never seen so terrible a face as that she showed him, with its wide eyes and blank, wet mouth.

"Give you away? Who? Who? Sam Booth? Slippery Sam give you away?"

"No—it wasn't Slippery Sam. He's been quite nice to me lately. It was that loony boy, Sing-a-song Joe they call him. He gave 'em the office. Put that nasty, superior kind o' copper, Gossett —you know him—on to it. Slippery Sam tried to stop it, but Gossett was too quick for him. Said that Sing-a-song Joe done it to help you. Dunno what he's talking about. What you staring at like that?"

"Oh, God! My pal! Done for by my pal!"

"Done for? Here, girl, don't take on so. It ain't so bad, perhaps. There'll be a bit o' money for you to go with. I oughta known it was bound to come. If it hadn't come that way, it'd a-come by Slippery Sam. He found out about it a week or two ago. I've had to keep him quiet with money, but he wasn't satisfied with money. He's bin askin' me for all sorts of things. Things I'd never think of giving him. Bluebell, girl, it's just as well, perhaps, that I'm in for it, and don't have to think over what he wanted. Now that this has happened he can't bother us no more. Bluebell—he was asking me for *you*."

"Yes? That's what makes it more awful. That Sing-a-song should have done this—now. 'Cos, you see, dad"—the words dropped hard and black from her lips—"you see, to save you, I gave myself to Slippery Sam last night."

Out of the quiet evening came the long scream of a tin whistle, as Sing-a-song pranced about the alleys, warm with the thought of service done to his lady.

A FAMILY AFFAIR

— VII —

A FAMILY AFFAIR

THERE was trouble down our street. There was something doing. There was a large fly in the sweet ointment of its social life. The wind was well up. And all along of that there little Connie Raymond and them there dirty Chinks. You could see at a glance that something was "up," for Mrs. Raymond was leaning across the sill of her open parlour window, which gave directly to the street; and Mrs. Raymond only sat in her parlour on solemn occasions, and only once before—when Aunt Polly upset the lamp—had the window been opened.

She was haranguing her two sons, Alf and Bert, who stood outside, smoking nonchalant cigarettes: Alf incipiently pugnacious; Bert, with a taste for diplomacy, thinking hard. A group of little girls gathered at a respectful distance, and sympathisers stood at their doors; for it was felt that the affront fell not only upon the Raymond family, but upon the whole colony of Nugget Street. And they listened and nodded as Mrs. Raymond made her jeremiad.

"To think of it. Our Connie. Going with a Chink. And ev'body in the place knowing it. Alwis kep' ourselves respectable we 'ave. On'y twice in 'is life was yer father put away. And you boys ain't on'y bin pinched oncer twice. Come to that— who ain't? Police trouble comes to ev'body—even the 'igh-up ones. But this—and with all the papers full o' stuff jus' now 'bout white gels going with Chinks, and 'ow it oughter be stopped. Goes and picks up one at that there Blue Lantern, and walks out with 'im. Night after night. It's enough to break yer 'eart. 'Er that I've kep' so respectable, too. Never bin anything like it in our family be- fore. All married fair and square, we was. And even if some of us picked wrong 'uns, leastways they was *white*. . . . Oh, don't stand there like a couple of lamp-posts. Say something!"

Alf looked at Bert, and Bert looked at his boots. Then Bill Higgins, the roadman, chipped in, and said something consolatory.

"I don't wonder yer worried, missus," said Bill Higgins.

"A nice gel like your Connie going with one o' them when she could 'ave the pick o' the street. It's shameful, that's what it is," said Bill Higgins.

"And o' them dirty yeller boys. They eats rats, y'know. Yerce, they do. I seen 'em. And worship images. And never wash theirselves. And treach- erous—yeh never know wher y'are with 'em. Stick a knife in yer back fer tuppence, and think nothing of it. And who knows where this might end?" said Bill Higgins.

"They might get 'old of Connie, and get 'er to one o' their dens, and you never see 'er again. Such things 'ave 'appened. Treat women worse'n dogs, they do. No reverence or respect for 'em. If Connie was a gel o' mine," said Bill Higgins, "and I caught 'er going with one of 'em, I'd flay 'er alive, I would."

Mrs. Raymond "Ooo'd" at the reference to a knife, and Alf and Bert turned on the intruder. "Life and soul o' the party, yew are, aincher? When we want your advice, we'll send a post card—see? 'Oppit!"

Higgins removed himself, and Alf and Bert looked at one another again. Mrs. Raymond repeated herself. "Well, what yeh going to do about it? Do *something*. It's fer you to up'old the good name of the family."

Alf turned back his cuffs and spat on his hands. "I'll show yeh what I'm going to *do*. Just lemme get 'old of the badstud fer five mintes. I'll——"

Mrs. Raymond sniffed. "Much better get 'old of 'er first, and find out 'ow far it's gone. She won't listen to 'er mother. She may take more notice of you."

"Well, Bert," said Alf, "you get 'old of 'er, and ask 'er——"

"No, you're the eldest. It'd come better from you."

"No, *you*," said Alf emphatically. "I spoke to 'er before—about that business of Aunt Amy's tomatoes. And she likes you better'n me."

"Well, as you spoke before, you ought to now. She'll take it better, being the second time. She ain't likely to give you another eye like the one——"

"Look 'ere, you're the talking man. If you're afraid of the gel, say so."

"Don't be silly. I ain't afraid of no gel."

"Well, I am. Of *'er*. So that's that. I ain't one fer words. I'm a man of action. I can't deal with women. But I can with men—if you can call a Chink a man. There won't be nothing said when I get 'old of 'im. There won't be much left of 'im—not enough to attract gels, anyway."

Bert spread his hands. "Ah, that's where you're wrong. You can't deal with these people that way. You wanter use tact. You gotter make 'em understand the situation. You can't settle everything with a punch on the jaw. We gotter get him to see the principle of the thing. A few words from me——"

"I'll make 'im see a lot o' things besides principles when I——"

Mrs. Raymond lamented with her hands. "Well, don't stand there nagging at one another. Do something."

"Well," said Alf, "we're going to. But I suppose the first thing to do is to find 'im."

"Yerce," said Bert pleasantly, "that'd be a good idea to start wiv, Brainy. As you're the man of action, it'll be your move."

"But aincher going to say a word to Connie about—— 'Ush! 'ere she comes."

Mrs. Raymond withdrew her head from the window-frame, and Alf and Bert looked up and down the street, and at their boots, and flourished their cigarettes and whistled. Through the doorway of the Raymond home stepped Miss Raymond, with the flourish of a young bird trying its wings. She stepped into the evening as though the evening had been "arranged" as a background from her. She passed her two brothers with a non-committal nod, which they affected not to see. Her mother glowered at her back. As she swam down the street, Alf nudged Bert.

"Now's the chance. She's going to meet 'im. If we follow 'em until she leaves 'im, and then follow 'im, we can get 'im down a back-way, and 'ave 'im to ourselves, eh?"

Bert agreed, and imparted the plan to Mrs. Raymond, who passed it to the street; and away went the two champions of tender white womanhood against the wiles of the crawling reptiles of Pennyfields. And there was still greater excitement down our street when it became known that the two young

Raymonds were about to enter Chinatown and track down the assaulter of their dignity, and work white justice upon a Chink. They were "seen off," as it were. They were given a valedictory ovation. It was as though the loungers said amiably among themselves: "Well, we shan't see *them* no more." Tales were told to Mrs. Raymond of the things that had been done to white men who had crossed the path of the Chinks; and she became again voluble.

"Ah, that's just what they are—like cats. I seen 'im 'anging about the end of the street for 'er, and 'e fair frightens me—the look of 'im. Just like a cat. You can't tell what 'e's thinking about. And you 'ear so much about this White Slave business now—it gives you the jumps."

And Alf and Bert, conscious of the deep adventure to which they were committed, swaggered as they departed.

And all this trouble down our street over a sentimental interlude produced by an idle moment and the weather. It was late summer, the season of languid skies; the time of appointments in the dusky public gardens; when shadowy faces at street corners greet shadowy passers; when streets, meagre and tattered by day, assume a chubby, self-satisfied air by night; when, in the chilly twilight, all is blurred like a worn-out film, and, in the Essex fields beyond Barking, the corn stands as yellow as the hair of the Blue Lantern's barmaid. It was at one dim corner of West India Dock Road, on such an evening, that the young Quong Foo filled his eye with the speaking face of little Connie Raymond. She called him with a smile, the smile of her age and class. It was not a happy smile, or a shy smile, or a satisfied smile, or a coy smile, but a wide, chill, masterful smile, to which he had no defence. Connie was an early adept in the technique of the game: she had a keen sense of the streets. As she stood negligently shouldering the corner of the alley, her flippant frock, that hung midway between knee and shoe, her saucy hat and blown brown hair could hardly fail to capture the heart of a bored exile. They did capture him; and Quong Foo and she walked together, and took a drink together at the Blue Lantern, and again walked together.

That was all. Connie Raymond, the accomplished little flirt, had walked out some evenings with a grave and courteous Chink, putting herself in the way of any little tricks he choose to work upon her. Asking for it, in fact. And because of this, a pogrom was proclaimed against the Oriental colony of Limehouse, and Alf and Bert were about to open it.

Near Limehouse Church they observed the meeting of Connie and her yellow boy, and each fortified the other with pronouncements of anathema upon all races that were not white of skin.

"Don't it make yer blood boil, Bert?"

"Not 'alf it don't. Disgusting, I call it."

"There ain't a name for it."

"I dunno. The papers what 'ave bin writing about Chinks getting 'old of white gels found all sorts o' names for it. Fancy names."

"I dessay. But the thing's bad enough wivout giving it a name. 'Ere they are in our country, making free wiv everything, and—— Ow, I can 'ardly keep me 'ands orf 'im."

"Ah, but you got to 'old yesself in. It don't *do.* Not with them. We gotter 'andle it delicate-like. Wotter we going to say when we first pick 'im up?"

"*Say?* I ain't going to say nothing. I thought you was going to do the talking."

"Yerce; but we got to interduce the subject, like. You know—polite but firm. The velvet 'and in the mailed fist."

"I should feel inclined to interduce the subject with me boot."

"Ah, but—s'pose 'e didn't take no notice of yer boot? Eh? You gotter be careful, y'know. They're crafty devils. Up to everything. S'pose while you're lifting yer boot 'e did something behind yer back. Yeh never know. That's why I believe in diplomatics."

"Rot! You take 'em too seriously. A pack o' dirty Chinks. We gotter teach 'em a lesson—show 'em they can't come messing round white gels. They

gotter be taught their place. I reckon I'm a match
for any three of them. They're yeller, and I'm
white—and I'm dam well going to let 'em know it."

"Shut up," said Bert. "Look—she's leaving 'im.
Come in this shop 'ere. You buy something, and
I'll watch."

They entered a small tobacconist's, and Bert
peeped from the door, and saw Connie mount an
east-bound bus, and the Chink walk leisurely down
West India Dock Road.

"Come on, Alf!"

They scampered out, and followed hotly.
"Damn! 'E's going right down to the Causeway.
We shan't get no chance to get 'im down an alley.
Never mind—we gotter go through with it."

"Don't you worry," said Alf. "I'll see this
through. Quick—'e's gorn down Pennyfields."

They trotted after the unsuspecting philanderer,
saw him in Pennyfields, and saw him enter a diminu-
tive shop. Swiftly they came up, and paused to
look at the place. Its front was encrusted with dirt;
its windows were dim with the smokes of many
months. It was more unkempt, more blear of aspect,
even more beset by evil odours than any house
in their own street. Behind the window was a litter
of tinned fruits and a few strips of fish. The wood-
work of the shop was discoloured by the flight of
ages. About it twined a filigree of spider's web.

"Huh!" said Alf. "So this is where 'e lives. And

to think of anybody out o' this dirty, stinking yellow
place coming after a white gel. And our sister, Bert,
our sister—eh?"

Bert was fired equally with indignation. "You're
right, Alf. Well, now, you wait outside, and I'll
go in. I know the kind of lingo they understand,
and if talk don't 'ave no effect on 'im, or if 'e tries
to do the dirty, you come in and put it across 'im.
See?"

So Bert dashed in, determined to stand no non-
sense from eaters of dog. He looked about the
dusty, airless shop, but saw no sign of the elegant
yellow dude. He was beginning to wonder if he
had mistaken the doorway, when a curtain at the
back of the shop was pulled aside, and an elderly
Chinaman, wearing a tattered canvas suit and steel
spectacles, came forward.

"Oh, ah—er—me wantum Chinkie just come in."

The old man regarded him gravely, without expression, as though waiting for him to speak. This
disconcerted the diplomatist, and he repeated himself.

"Me wantum Chinkie just come in. Me wantum
talkee young Chinkie."

"Do I understand that you wish to speak to
Quong Foo?"

Bert looked sharply at the old man, ready to per-
ceive trickery in every movement.

"Me not know 'is name. Me wantee Chinkie just

come in. Chinkie come muchee talkee-talkee my sister—savvy? Chinkie go walkee-walkee my sister.
Me wantum talkee Chinkie."

The old man removed his spectacles and regarded
Bert with cold eyes. Then he spoke in a polished
English accent.

"Ah. I am the father of Quong Foo. I believe
he is the young man you speak of. Do I understand
that you are the brother of that white girl with
whom I have seen my son walking."

"That's me." The cold precision of the old man's
language drove Bert back from pidgin to Cocknese.
"And I've come to see about it. A yeller man and
a white gel. It's gotter stop."

"I see. And you have come to treat in the matter? Very well. How much?" He held out a
wrinkled hand.

"Eh?"

"How much?" The question put Bert at a loss.
He went to the door and drew Alf into consultation.
" 'E says 'Ow much?' 'E's the bloke's father."

Alf clutched the doorway for support. " 'Ow
much? Meaning money? I'll give 'im 'ow much.
It's blackmail, that's what it is. Blackmail, Bert.
I'll give 'im——" He dashed into the shop with
hands ready for use.

"What's this you're giving us, Chinkie?"

The old man held out a hand, with a question:
"Five pounds?"

"Five pounds? *F-five—p-p-pounds?*"   Alf and
Bert stared.   Alf spluttered, and made rude noises.
"Well, of all the bleedun impudence!   A dirty yeller
Chink to—— Look 'ere!"—and Alf delivered that
paralysing and, to most people, unanswerable question: "Who th'ell d'yeh think *yew* are?   Your
blinking son'll be dam lucky if 'e gets orf wiv a mouf
to eat wiv, time I've done wiv 'im.   Mucking round
white gels—in our country, too.   And then working
blackmail on it.   Five pounds?   Understand this,
Mister Chinkie.   We ain't offering no bribes in this
business.   We don't ave to.   Five *pounds?*   We're
English, and you're yeller.   You're in England, and
you gotter be'ave yesselves as such—see?   See that
bunch of fives?"   He held up a knotted fist.   "It's
made better men than you or your son spit out their
ivories.   White men, too.   If you bring that son
of yours out here, I'll learn 'im what it means
to——"

Across Alf's phillipic cut the stern voice of the
Chink: "I fear I am not sufficiently acquainted with
the idiom of your language to follow all your remarks.   I gather only that the mention of five pounds
arouses your indignation.   Therefore, to settle the
matter quickly, I will overlook any question of an
apology for the affront, and will give ten, twenty,
if need be fifty pounds if you will remove this
white woman of your low-born family from my son's
neighbourhood and undertake that she shall at no

time again seek him out and disgrace the honourable house of Quong by association with its upright son."

And then there was silence: Alf and Bert recognised, for the first time, that there are some situations to which neither words nor blows are adequate.

THE LITTLE FLOWERS OF FRANCES

VIII

THE LITTLE FLOWERS OF FRANCES

THEY'RE a sorry crowd, the reg'lars of the Blue Lantern. Even the brightest of them, the flash boys and girls, carry their terribly new store clothes with a bedraggled air. The others are nakedly downcast, without clothing of bravado to cover them or weapon of spirit to arm them.

The Blue Lantern stands on Chinatown corner, where the missionaries love to prowl. It is kept by an ex-bruiser known to his reg'lars as Dickery Dock. It is to Limehouse what the village green is to the rural community. It is the centre of past history and of current endeavour. In its bars new friendship are formed, and old scores bloodily wiped out. There hot, hard words and vociferous debate lead to blows and the police court, or end, more ignobly, with shocking beer-shed.

There valorous schemes are laid, and the vain cunning of the police is with sharper cunning frustrated. There the keen wit of the Cockney meets the deceptive frankness of the Oriental and the tortuous reserve of the black, and is often bested.

Upon an evening of winter, when, in the mist, the substance of the streets melted into shadow, and shadow took on body, Dickery Dock looked about the house and stroked his chin with complacent gesture. At the same moment a policeman, trying to look like an ordinary citizen, looked in, and also made a complacent gesture. All the boys were there: vigilance could be relaxed for a while. Dick the Duke was there, with his usual crowd of worshipping ladies. There, too, were Binkie Flanagan, the auto-matic-machine expert, Nobby the Nark, Big Bessie, some of the Roseleaf Boys, old Quong Lee and John Sway Too, Flash Florrie, little Chrissie Rainbow, Greenstockings, and, in a corner, Sing-a-song Joe, the loony. All the reg'lars, in short, replenishing from pewter pot and uncouth glass their store of hope and enterprise, and recovering that calm acceptance of the untoward which men call philosophy. As the rattle of coins on the counter increased, so did the buzz and clatter of the saloon and four-ale bars gather volume. Listening from without, the stranger would have said that everybody within was happy. Their noise flowed to the street like the quiet gurgle of a self-satisfied stream: a stream that ignores in its careless passage the muddy bed above which it flows.

But one among the reg'lars was not happy; could not even borrow an hour's delight on the usury of the glass. Frances of the Causeway, described

colloquially as "Fanny, poor kid," sat alone on a
bench, face and hands listless. Although sitting
with the crowd, she had dropped the mask of alert
nonchalance assumed by girls of her class in public
places: the strain of carrying it was too severe for
her worn nerves. In the last two days she had
realised that she was a back number. Such beauty
as she had once had was now obliterated. Her
hair was thin and colourless. Her face no longer
took aptly the emmolients and powders that she
applied. It was becoming an effort to be skittish
and effervescent in the presence of potential customers. She was no longer facile in dalliance; her
profane comment no longer came pat to the occasion.
Even the black men about the streets failed to
look twice at her.

She sat "all-gone," as she would have expressed
it. The bright light of invitation that customarily
sat on her face, once assumed as a trade trick, later
to become habitual, was out, and the coarse face
hung empty. But in every line of the flagging figure
was written disgust and yearning. She was done,
and she knew it; and she held yet enough of her
first girlhood's love of the good and the seemly
to suffer disgust at her situation and impotent desire
to amend it.

Others had played her game, and had done well
out of it. Some had married Chinks, and now led
silken lives, with flowered temples made to their

honour. Others had moved up west, where they had found sleek protectors and had put money in the bank. Others had married seamen or small tradesmen. All had been careful where she had been gay, spending money as she got it and financing men friends when they were hard up. Little Chrissie would not be that sort of fool. She was in the game for solid reward, and saw that she got every promised penny out of it. Greenstockings, too, knew where to draw the line between frivolity in business hours and recklessness in leisure. But Fanny had been caught by the festal side of the life and the loud company, and had crowded a jag into every hour.

And now she was through, and they talked of her. "Whassup with Fanny, poor kid?" asked Greenstockings. "Looks as though she'd drawn the winner and lorst the brief."

"I dunno. Seems to 'ave got the fantods lately. No doing nothing with 'er. She can't get the boys now, and when she told me she was 'ard up, and I told 'er she ought to go to the Mission Workers, and they'd get 'er an honest job, she fair snapped my 'ead orf. Fact is, she's made a mess of things. She didn't ought never to 'ave bin in this game. She ain't fit for it. She's too—you know—too— thinks too much, like. She's told me. Although she's done things I'd never do, she ain't comfortable. Keeps on thinking of what she's done. She ought to 'ave bin respectable, reely. She's made for that. Can't you see 'er bathing the baby and getting 'er old man's dinner? She ain't cut out for this. She's let it get 'old of 'er too much."

Fanny sat brooding. A young seaman, in neat, shore-going clothes, brought a drink from the counter, and sat down near her. He glanced at her; then edged away. She caught the glance and returned it, not professionally, but with appeal. She leaned towards him.

"Lend us 'alf-a-crown, boy."

He looked up again; edged a little farther away; then turned a shoulder and bent to his glass, awkwardly, as one afraid of such women while afraid of not behaving like a man of the world.

"Lend us a shilling, then."

He became confused; remembered an appointment; drank up and departed.

Dickery Dock, seeing that she was without a drink, called to her: " 'Ave a drink, Fanny?"

She went over to the bar. "No, thanks; I don't want a drink. I say, lend us half-a-crown, Dickery."

"Lend you 'alf-a-crown? 'Ere—come orf it. This ain't a Finance and Mortgage Corporation. You can 'ave a drink on the 'ouse, if yeh like, but——"

"No, I want money."

"Money? Well, I don't know what yer chances are o' gettin' money 'ere. Where's yer security?

Where are *you* going to get money—now? You ain't got nothing to sell now, Fanny. You realise that yesself, doncher? You're past it. No, Fan, you ain't got no chance with the boys about 'ere against little Cherry and young Greenstockings and the other flappers. No, kid, you'll alwis be welcome to a drink 'ere, but money's another matter. You know I make it a rule never to lend money. I don't mind sticking up a drink when a chap's 'ard up, but lend 'em money to spend in other 'ouses —no."

"I don't want it to spend in other 'ouses."

"Wodyeh want it for, then?"

"I'm going away, an' I want to buy something most particular."

"Going away? Well, if you ain't the bleedun limit! Wanter borrow money to go *away* with! You take the 'Untley and Palmer, you do. No, Fan, I'm sorry, but I 'ardly think that security would be good enough even for Mugg from Mugtown. 'Ave a drink."

"No, thanks. **I'll go.** Where I won't bother nobody."

She turned from the bar, her face momentarily expressing chagrin until its lines deepened into utter misery. The landlord looked after her, puzzled at her attempt to break his rules, and at her attitude. As she crept through the swing doors, he looked at some of the boys standing at the bar. " 'Ear what she said? I think she wants watching. 'Where I won't bother nobody,' she said. See if you can find old Nobby, and get 'im to keep an eye on 'er. She looks as if she's got something in 'er 'ead—making a 'ole in the water, or some idea of that sort. She better be looked after. We don't want another scandal round this 'ouse, just on top o' the last."

They dug out Nobby, and dispatched him on his errand; and the beer engines banged and hissed, and the cash register clattered and rang, and the turmoil of glass and voice rose with the rising hands of the clock.

At half-past nine Nobby returned. He sat down on the lounge, and his shoulders and stomach vibrated and bass rumbles came from him. Nobby was laughing. He always laughed privately, within himself; but in the communism of the public-house private laughter is frowned upon. There men abide by the wisdom of the poet—that the weary old earth is in need of your mirth, it has enough grief of its own.

"Now come on, Nobby, spit it out. Let's 'ave the joke. Don't keep it all to yesself."

"G-get us a d-drink, someone. Bitter. I was laughing," he jerked from tremulous lips, "I was laughing at Fanny, poor kid. She's just bin nabbed."

"Nabbed?" snapped Dickery Dock. "Whaffor?

She ain't bin an'——" He looked up and his great eyes rolled in elephantine agitation.

"No. Pinching—p-pinching f-flowers!"

"Pinching flowers? Shurrup!"

"True's I sit 'ere. Pinching a fourpenny bunch o' lilies-o'-the-valley from old Gorton's shop, an' old Gorton caught 'er at it, an' 'anded 'er over."

"Well, it sounds queer, but I don't see nothing to laugh about like you're laughing."

" 'Tain't the pinching—though that's funny. It's what she said when they arst 'er why she done it. Wod yeh think she said? Our Fanny, mindyer. Frances of the Causeway—knowing 'er and 'er ways as we do. Wod yeh think she said?"

"Go on. What?"

"Said she pinched 'em 'cos she 'adn't got no money and wanted 'em bad. Said she was fed up with things and was going to end it, and wanted the flowers 'cos—'cos a bad girl like 'er couldn't go before God with nothing in 'er 'and. Fanny, mind yeh! Talk about laugh!"

But Landlord Dickery Dock was indignant. "Laugh! I can't see nothing to laugh abaht. Seems to me solemn-like. 'Tain't no laughing matter— *pore gell*"

THE PERFECT GIRL

IX

THE PERFECT GIRL

IT is one of the little tales of John Sway Too, which he tells at evenings to his wandering fellows in the half-lit room behind his store in Poplar High Street. There, amid the pungent odours of suey sen and jagree dust and unguents, tempered by the sweeter essence of areca nut, gather the youthful yellow seamen newly come to London. There, from the venerable lips of John Sway Too, they learn Rules of Conduct for this strange land and gather much entertainment besides, for John Sway Too has seen the passing of many seasons under the steel skies of Limehouse.

"It is to be observed," he remarked one evening to a semicircle of young admirers, "that the white daughters of this stream which men call the Thames, by whose banks we now sojourn, are very apt in guile."

"Ao!" cried the company in chorus.

"And now that statements of a highly objectionable nature are daily being made in the bazaars and in the printed leaves by the men of this land against the association of their daughters with the serene and refined ones from the land of the White Poppy, this person who addresses you would advise you all to abjure the company of the white maidens."

He paused to reach from a shelf a jar of li-un, and extract a portion of its contents with his yen-hok.

"The refined assembly," he continued, "will doubtless refrain from expressions of displeasure, and will concede from their own experience that the words of this person are weighted with wisdom when he tells them that the attraction which they possess for these white maidens is almost wholly in proportion to the number of taels—or, as the barbarian tongue has it, Bradburys—in their possession; whereby the maidens may be afforded refined and polished relaxation in tea-houses and theatres."

The company looked doubtfully around the room and about the floor, but none met the eye of his fellows or the eye of John Sway Too.

"Nevertheless," continued the narrator complacently, "I have myself found one white maiden of these cold streets—a maiden of surpassing virtue and of beauty like to dew upon chrysanthemums. Fairer than the Great Night Lantern on the garden is she; kinder than the sun to the bursting bud; sweetest than the rain to the parched fields; more gracious than the nest to the tired bird."

"Hi-yah!" cried his audience. "Will not the estimable John Sway Too tell us of her?"

John Sway Too took the portion of li-un into his hand and rubbed it slowly into a pellet; and the company drew closer.

"It was about the time of Clear Weather," he began, "when, in our country, the almond blossom is scattering its colour about the garden walks, and the swallow comes again; when, beneath the brown earth begin those agreeable stirrings that rise at last to the full laughter of the harvest; when, beneath the bosoms of refined youths such as those I now see before me, begin these not unpleasing tremors that come at last to harvest in a kiss. I had, on a fair evening of this season, followed my custom of visiting a tea-house within this street, and there engaging myself with white men in a game of fan-tan. But upon that evening some evil spirit was in possession of the cards, and all my skill could not prevent my losing many cash to my base associates. At a point when but a few cash were left to me, I resolved to play one game more, believing that my unremitting devotion to my ancestors would lead them to intervene on behalf of their miserable son. The agreeable state of mind with which I entered upon this game was, however, violently displaced by emotions of the most agitating nature; for I soon observed that the cards which had fallen to my hand were intolerably inadequate to the purpose of recovering any portion of my coins. When, therefore, the game was well begun, I contrived, by that dexterity which my dignified father had passed to me as his highest gift, to thwart the evil spirit that sought to undo me, and to substitute, by a rapid movement of the arm, five cards of high value, which I carried always in my tunic as a charm against evildoers, for those then in my hand.

"But alas! misfortune pursues even those most attentive to the Four Books and most devout in service to their ancestors. Scarce had I effected the substitution, when the pig-like eye of the wholly detestable Bill Hawkins perceived the movement; and, disregarding all the laws of the Book of Rites, he cried aloud his discovery in that voice which many have likened to the filing of an iron chain by a number of watermen under the influence of rice spirit. Immediately the assembled company laid aside their dignity, and fell upon me with blows and base comments upon my accomplished father and the method by which he bred me. With a total loss of the perpendicular, I was hurried from the tea-house to the Causeway, and there subjected to usage of a degrading and highly painful nature.

"Suddenly, at a point when the repeated blows had become well-nigh unbearable, they ceased, and a silence fell upon my persecutors; and there appeared in our midst a white maiden of loveliness surpassing any loveliness that this person had at any time conceived. Dazed as I was by my brutal treatment, I was yet swift to note how my heart leapt and cried at sight of her. Dense dark hair with the sheen of water at midnight, streamed about her milk-white brow. Whiter than the blossom of the cherry were her hands, and her eyes shone with the lights of a thousand festival lanterns. The running lines of her limbs were as happy to the eye as the flashing curves of the swallow in the middle air; and through the dusk her face glowed like an evening water-lily.

"While I lay prone on the hard road, she addressed high words to my tormentors, and her bright hands flashed against them like fire-flies; and I felt that sweeter to my wounds than all ointments and dressings would be one caress from those hands. And lo! when she had made an end of speaking, my persecutors crept sadly away, and she bent to me —to this utterly degraded and altogether insignificant person—and placed an arm about me, and helped me to a position of dignity. Like a roll of silk was her arm, and my heart became as the sun at high noon. I murmured foolish words to her, not thanking her as my rescuer, but blessing her for the touch of her hands and for her gracious presence; blessing her for her beauty and for that I was vouchsafed to gaze upon her.

"Then she led me away to her palace. I have wandered much about these parts, alongside this

stream, but in all my wanderings had found nothing
but the large, ungainly buildings of the merchants
and the disreputable hovels where dwell the mean
and the base of this city. Scarce, however, had we
made one turn out of the Causeway, than we came
upon a noble and dignified mansion, with iron gates,
tiled paths, and a green door. By means of a key
this maiden of surpassing loveliness opened the
green door and motioncd me to enter. With
trembling limbs, partly due to the vile treatment
to which I had been subjected, and partly due to
the mystery and enchantment of her presence, I
did so. When she had made light, she illuminated
two lanterns, and I found myself walking upon soft
rugs in a chamber garnished with flowers and silks.
Bidding me rest upon a purple couch, she retired;
and presently returned with soft water and
unguents, and with these she blessed my bruises—
ay, with those lily hands she tended me. While I
lay there in all my baseness and misery, this white
maiden soothed and caressed my hurt places, and
fed my bosom with the rich light of her eyes. When
I was fully comforted, she brought me wine and
sweet foods, and sat by me as I ate, and ate with me,
and my heart grew so light as I received her smiles
that I scarce knew it was there; nay, it had changed,
I think, into a little murmurous song or a soft flower
of the springtide.

"The hours grew to the noon of night. Yet I

moved not. I could not move, for her beauty held
me in delicious bonds. As she sat by me, my heart
danced with the fumes of the time of Clear Weather,
and little white thoughts flowed and fluttered between our hearts, and the room was sweetened by
them. My offending fingers wandered through the
forest of her hair. Her lucid face was a field for
my eyes to rove in. In my arms I held her, heart
to heart, and all her shining loveliness was mine.
Her soft robes ran through my fingers, and the strip
of lace about her neck was to me fairer than the
jewels of the temple. When the lanterns faded,
her eyes flooded the night with silver, and with
my head upon her young breast I dreamed of these
streets in Limehouse, and how all men were kind
to us; where white maidens scoffed not at us because
our faces are golden like the sun; nor deceived us
with soft words for the purpose of obtaining taels
from us.

"To me, John Sway Too, she gave these hours
of beauty. But she gave me more than this. She
gave me her inner mind. She gave me kindness
and warm understanding; and though our spoken
words fell without significance upon each other's
ears, we had full knowledge without them. So
passed the hours in the bliss of sympathy and beauty.
All these gifts I had of her without return. Nay,
far from requiring money of me for the gift her
charms, as other white girls do, she gave me of

her own store—pressed it upon me that I might replenish my purse by play.

"Yea, truly, when at last I felt that I should depart, she pressed upon me many taels, knowing that I was without substance, and a basket of elegant provisions. When I would have made a dignified refusal, she smiled upon me, and I then took what she had offered me and knew that I need speak no words of thanks. She led me herself from her own noble mansion to the door of my base and despicable hovel; and there, in the street, she left me with a memory of love that scattered wonder and beauty upon the mean houses about me, and made even the shadows of the shops that fell upon the pathway she had trodden, more dear and desirable than all the substance of my own country."

John Sway Too paused, and reached for his pipe, while the company sat mute with shining eyes and gaping mouths.

Presently—"And did you never see her again—this maiden of surpassing virtue and loveliness?" asked one.

"Many times since have I seen her, my son. And each time she is more lovely and gracious, and pours sweeter blessings upon my unworthy person."

"Ao! Ao!" they cried eagerly. "She is still here then? She is still to be seen about these streets? Could it be granted that we might at some time catch even a distant glimpse of her enchantments—could for one moment behold her?"

"In truth, yes. More than that, you may see her and be with her even as I have been with her. You may feast of her white beauty and rare mind even as I."

"Hi-yah! Where, oh, where may we find her, O refined and elegant John Sway Too. Tell us quickly. Direct us to her, to this one white maid who will not scorn our worship."

"The gracious and high-minded company," replied John Sway Too, "who have listened so attentively to my trivial and wearisome discourse, may find the Perfect White Maid even as I found her; and once they have found her they will renounce the company of all other daughters of this sunless land. They will find her in anyone of these little pellets of li-un which I am about to smoke in this very ordinary and ill-constructed pipe."

THE AFFAIR' AT THE WAREHOUSE

THE AFFAIR AT THE WAREHOUSE

IT is a pitiful story, this of George and Violet. Silly, I call it. Motiveless. To young lives pulled about, and the ends twisted into nothing. Nobody to blame. All doing the right thing, as they saw it. But that's the way of things.

Commercial Road East is a loud London thoroughfare, packed with poor shops and stalls. In it the modern jostles the antique, and the antique shames the modern. A few tawdry cinemas throw upon it a thin festal glow. It links Whitechapel with Limehouse. So well acquainted are its people, with petty crime and rough justice that the discovery of the bodies in the warehouse made little impression upon them save as a topic for the evening in the bars. Three days after the inquest it was forgotten. Here are copied the few surviving documents by which the story became public.

. . . .

Well Joe this is a hell of a thing to do, but we are going through with it. I was called up last week. But I am not going and I cant go till me and Violet have had a bit of time together. Aint it awful we should be like this—always at someones beck and call. Oh Joe love does make a difference to you. I hope some day you will find a girl—not like what we used to click with in Commercial Road but a real girl. Violet was 15 on Tuesday, so we decided to make it that day. I met her as she come from the factory Joe and we went a long walk and then a tram ride and then got back these parts about midnight. I had got it all fixed. I had been looking round for some time and found what we wanted where nobody would ever dream of looking for us. It was a warehouse Joe over in the Island but it had been empty for a long time. I had got in the night before and had a look round and it was all nice and dry on the first floor and I found a lot of straw shavings and things and I made up a bit of a bed like and tied a lot of it together and made hassicks to sit on and I fixed up a few old planks to make a sort of table. Lucky it was warm weather else we should have been cold because it wouldnt have done to have started a fire in the stove because someone who knew the place might see the moke coming out. Well Joe that is where I took her. I had laid in a bit of grub of a sort and at one in the morning we sat down there together as cosy as you please and had it. We didnt neither of us eat much. We was too excited I think.

Oh Joe we was happy. I hope Joe some day you will be as happy because you have been a good pal to me and I always liked you Joe and I want everybody to know how happy you can be together with a girl you love and what loves you. Oh Joe I never knew before how beautiful things were. I never knew how lovely girls are and what a difference comes into a girls face when she looks at her boy and nestles up to him. Joe do you remember how we used to joke about love and getting married. Its seems horrible to thing of it now. But I hope Joe you wont have to hide like a rabbit and only slink out at night all because you love somebody—that is what we got to do.

.   .   .   .   .   .

DEAR JOE—we have been here twenty-four hours now. I suppose V has been missed from the factory and from home and I reckon they are wondering where I got to but I know you wont give a pal away Joe.

I slipped out last night to get some more grub in. Good job the streets is dark. Anyhow I didnt show my face at any shop round here. I went up to Canning Town. I couldn't get much because we darent use our ration books us being registered at local shops for this and that which would have got us nabbed if we shown our faces where we was known. But I called at Fat Freds place up at Canning Town and got some boiled beef and pease from him without a coupon. I pumped him a bit and he didnt know anything was wrong. There wont be nothing in the papers for a bit I suppose but I bet V's father will go to the police if she aint home to-night. I managed to get some beer and some lemonade and I pinched a glass from the lemonade shop.

Oh Joe when I got back I slipped in quiet like and V didnt hear me and what do you think I saw. She was sitting on one of the hassicks and just as I got there she reached for my old cap—what I thought I hadnt better wear because it is a bright brown colour and might be known—and hugged it to her and kissed it. Oh Joe I cant tell you what it makes a chap feel when he sees his girl do like that. As soon as I see what she was doing I slipped out again and come back again and made a bit of a noise this time so she would know. Oh Joe how I love her. Joe if we was to die at the same time I want you to go to her people and mine and make them swear to let us be buried together. You will do this for me Joe wont you. You wont let a pal down will you. You got to do it in case anything happens.

I expect her father wont half be wild but if it did happen you must tell him it is my wish and V's wish. It is a bit out of the ordinary I know but if he loved his daughter and wants to do something to make up for those awful bruises that she carries on her arms and legs from him I think he will agree

to it. If he doesnt and there is a Judge above us
I hope he will meet out punishment to those what
have deserved it by keeping us apart and treating
her so shameful. Tell him that Joe.

But why am I going on like this. We are just
in love with everything at present and we both
laugh a lot at having to sneak out and lie doggo
all day. I took V out for a stroll at about eleven
and we mooched round a bit and it was a lovely
night. Although we dont talk to nobody but each
other we aint lonely. You aint Joe when you love
properly.

.   .   .   .   .   .

Well Joe last night we skipped away about eleven
and it was another lovely night so we walked to
Liverpool Street. We caught a late train. I didnt
know where it was going but we hopped on without
a ticket and went miles and miles into the country.
And when it stopped at a place that looked nice we
got out and I paid the fares from Liverpool Street.
It was lovely. We got there about one in the morning and we walked a bit of a way till we come to a
wood and then we laid down under a tree where it
was all mossy and soft and we woke up about six
when it was light and it looked just like God's own
country—all lovely. V did enjoy it. Well we just
lazed about in them woods and played hide and seek
and run races. Come on says V come and catch me.
And off she went and she can run too. She did lead

me a dance. And then she bolted into another wood. I was yards behind her and there I heard her voice saying I am lost come and find me. So I went after where the noise come from and then I heard it behind me—I am lost come and find me. And then I seemed to hear it everywhere but when I went there it come from somewhere else. And all of a sudden Joe I felt so lonely like in that wood because I couldnt see her nowhere but only heard her saying come and find me. And I didn't like it. And I got tired of the wood. So I called to her come out and there she was right behind me. We didnt play that game no more. We was getting hungry. So we walked into a village and had a slap up time with eggs and tea and lettiss and radishes and things. There was a piano there and V sat down and played all the ragtimes for about an hour. She always was one for a bit of music as you know. The old girl who kept the place thought we was just a couple of London munition workers what had got a day off and she was so took with V she couldnt do enough for us. We had a fine wash and brush up there and wanted it. That is what troubles us most. We cant find not water in the warehouse. She said she could let us have rooms if we wanted to stay the night but me and V didnt want to be separated and we thought sleeping out nicer. So we slept out that night again but not in those woods because we found a nicer place just on the banks of a river.

V is no end tickled by the way I talked to the old girl and the way I manage things and find out the cheap places. She said she never knew I had so much swank in me that is because I have always been a bit quiet and awkward with her like a chap is when he is really in love.

.   .   .   .   .   .

We come back to the warehouse to-night. Everything looked alright. It didnt look as though anybody had spotted us. I wish there was some way of your dropping a note into the place so I can hear the news and know what is going on and whether there is any trouble about our going away. Joe that is quite right that about a friend in need being a friend indeed. You have always been the best pal a chap ever had and we have had some great times together aint we. You have been closer than a brother to me Joe. I will say that. You will easy know the place. Second to the right as you get into Folly Wall—a big empty place with a couple of pulley cranes outside and a notice to Let. Stick it under the door Joe but dont try to see us. We cant take no risks.

.   .   .   .   .   .

Got your note old man. I guessed how it would be but it is a good thing they don't put two and two together. I hope the police didnt upset my landlady when they called round. She is a good old body. I suppose they think I have just bolted

to avoid military service and dont guess we have
gone together. I cant help laughing at that when I
know how we was both looking forward to joining
up when we was eighteen wasnt we. But that was
before I met V. I am sorry her Dad has written to
the papers about her disappearance. I showed V
your note and she says she will never never go back
to her Dad. Oh Joe if you had seen the bruises
and weels on her dear body you would feel like I
do like as if I could do a murder on the man what
done it. Bad as things are when I see my little
white darling all marked like that and think of the
shame and torture that I have saved her from I
am glad over again for taking her away. As long
as we are not caught I dont care a dam whether
the whole world knows we have gone together. I
never did mind what people thought about me no
more do you. We have always kept ourselves to
ourselves havent we and V was always refined and
didnt mix much with the other lot and took no notice
what they said about her. She asks me to thank
you for what you have done for us and for keeping
our secret. You are the only man in the world beside
ourselves that knows. V never told a soul—she
hadnt got anybody she could trust like I can trust
you old man. One thing troubles me. When V
had read your letter and the bit about the cops being
after me she looked rather funny. She seems to be
happy enough and I think she is for God knows I

would cut my throat if that would make things any nicer for her. But she has said once or twice that she has been a lot of trouble to me and to everybody else and she said it again this time and I dont like to hear her talk that way. Oh Joe—what a wonderful girl she is. Such character and principals she has got—I never met anyone like her for that among our set which is all the kind I know. If ever there was a real good girl it is her. And so lively and all —over what we have to put up with in this place.

. . . . . .

Oh Joe Joe. It has happened. I knew it would. I never dared think of it. I never said so to myself. I just knew it deep down like. You will say that sounds silly but it is a fact. I knew it all the time. And it has come.

Joe I had been out to get something for supper and I come back with some hard-boiled eggs and some beer and a loaf of bread and some bananas and some saveloys what I had knocked off while the chap was arguing with someone. And I was looking forward to the feed we was going to have Joe—and oh Joe it is awful to write about. Me coming in with those things what I had had such fun in getting for her. And then Joe there she was lying on the bed of shavings all still. I knew before I looked at her. She was dead Joe and there was a bottle of something by her side. How she had got it I don't know because she never went

into any shop without me. She must have brought
it with her in case. But oh Joe she is dead now—
my darling little V. Oh God I loved her Joe more
than I thought one could and it is me what has
killed her. I didn't ought to have interfered. I
didn't ought to have taken her from her home but
what could I do Joe when I loved her so and see
her suffering like that. I never thought that being
in love meant what it has to me. I never see none
of these awful things coming Joe when I first knew
her. She had left a letter for me for good-bye.
This is what she says Joe my precious little girl:

SWEET,

I love you too much to see you in any more
trouble than you have already got into through
loving me so. I will now say good-bye sweetheart
for the last time and when you see Joe say Hullo
for me and tell him I hope we will all meet again
some day. You will let Dad know wont you sweetheart. I thought after a while we might have gone
back and got married when he had calmed down
a bit but there seems no way out.

Why cant we do what we want to so long as we
dont do nobody any harm. When I met you dear
I knew then that the world was good and all a
lovely place. Why did they bother us so. I wonder why we cant all be happy. I thought the world
was so big and good but really it is like being in

a cage. You cant do anything in the world unless somebody else lets you. I am myself and so are you. Why cant we be let alone.

Tell Joe that if he finds a nice girl I hope he wins her and dont have nobody saying you shant and he will be happy as I know I would if I could live for always with you dear.

Well Joe I want you to take this letter to the police and tell them to come here and they will find us because this is Goodbye for me too Joe. I cant help thinking as I write this and look at her lying there so still what she was saying in the woods. It seems I can hear her voice in this warehouse Joe saying I am lost come and find me. So I am going to her Joe. I got that little gun what we bought for a lark in Bethnal Green Road and I got two cartridges. Joe—dont you forget what I said in one of the other letters about our being side by side. You got to see it done Joe for the sake of your old dead pal. And now goodbye and all the best to you and all the rest of the chaps at the works. It is all over. It had to end somehow I suppose and I knew this would be it and perhaps this way is just as well. There is a lot of misery in the world Joe that nobody can help. My darling had a rough time all her life but she looks very quiet now like as though she had dropped

off to sleep after being very tired. I hope you will
have a better time when you meet your girl Joe.

.   .   .   .

From the Local Press.

When information was taken to Ephraim Carfax, who was found at the Wesleyan Chapel at
Foljambe Street, that the dead body of his daughter, Violet Beatrice Carfax, had been found in
a disused warehouse side by side with the dead
body of a man who was being sought by the military,
he made no comment beyond saying: "I thought
she had gone with a man. This is a sad blow.
What are they going to do with the bodies? I
suppose this will get into the papers." Mr. Carfax, who has an ironmongery business in Maroon
Street, is a well-known chapel worker, and is highly
respected in the district.

.   .   .   .

At the inquest on the bodies of Violet Beatrice
Carfax, 15, and George Borrowdale, 18, verdicts
of suicide while of unsound mind were returned in
each case, a rider being added to the effect that the
girl was clearly under the influence of the man at
the time. Letters from the deceased were put in
which seemed to call for no other verdict. The
father of the girl, giving evidence, stated that she
had disappeared on Wednesday the 18th. Regarding certain passages in the letters, he admitted
having frequently whipped her in order to stop her

from "going with boys," and to make her come in by nine o'clock. She was always in the streets. He was not aware that on several occasions when she had not come home until half-past ten, and had been punished, her factory was working overtime. He had not believed her when she pleaded this, as she was not always truthful.

The jury expressed their sympathy with the father in his bereavement, who is a prominent and highly-respected chapel worker.

.   .   .   .

The funeral of Violet Beatrice Carfax, who, to-gether with a man, committed suicide in a disused warehouse, took place to-day at Poplar. Although the deceased had expressed in their letters a wish that they might be buried together, the father of Carfax refused to permit this. The body of the man was interred to-day at Islington. There were no mourners in either case, Mr. Carfax, who is well known locally as a chapel worker, being confined to his home with a chill.

BIG BOY BLUE

BIG BOY BLUE

BIG BOY BLUE had been for some years the most adroit cop of his station. He was a good mixer. He had presence, carriage, and address, and could wear mufti without looking like a policeman. He was big, calm, taciturn; slow to speak, quick to smile; and in all situations imperturbable. The most exacting business, the cleanest skin-of-the-teeth extraction from disaster, seemed to afford him no thrill. If he discussed his adventures with others of his division, he did so perfunctorily, in flat tones, as though speaking of another. He seemed always the spectator, observing himself as well as others. He drank with his fellows, and received their confidences, giving nothing in exchange beyond a call for the next round. He seemed to stand aloof from the harmless human follies of his circle; was impervious to the beauty of girls; did not gamble; took little interest in games; did not tell the kind of anecdote that men tell one another; yet found himself welcome in any crowd.

His colleagues liked him; bar-tenders liked him; crooks liked him and stood him drinks and chaffed him about their mutual relationship. He was even welcome in Chinatown. Little misconduct took place in those streets while he was about. Whenever a Tong battle was imminent Big Boy Blue was told off to see to it; and he saw to it by walking up to the battling Chinks and calmly demanding their weapons; which were immediately given up to him.

At the Tea-house of Ah Fat he was notably welcome, and the best tea was served to him with selected chrysanthemum buds. He was welcome here for two reasons: because Mr. Ah Fat was wise in Western ways and had discovered the expediency of standing well with the police, and because Mr. Ah Fat had a daughter who, from her shuttered retreat, looked forth and worshipped the valiant form and grave demeanour of Big Boy Blue. Ah San Lee was so carefully guarded by her father that few knew of her existence. Seldom was she seen by strangers. On rare occasions, customers at her father's tea-house had seen, momentarily, at the end of the dim passage leading to the kitchen, a round, moonlike face with flat, black hair; but it was gone before one might say whether it belonged to man or woman.

But Boy Blue had seen her. When, on unpremeditated occasions, he had called at a late hour

at the shop of Ah Fat, and entered the rooms for
a tour of inspection, Ah Fat had received him
with courtesy; and, after the inspection, had pressed
upon him a pot of suey sen. Then he would ac-
company him to a table in the empty restaurant and
Ah San Lee would come forth and wait upon them.
The exquisite finish of her form and the grace of
her movements and her plaintive smile were lost
upon Boy Blue; he observed only men; and he
would talk to her, with tolerant, heavy humour, and
in the manner which some men think pleasing to
children.

"Well, Angel-Face, d'you back the winner yes-
terday? No? Come, come. And after what I
told you. I told you to back Ching-Chang for the
two-thirty." And: "Well, Gladiola, when are
you going to grow up and get as big as me, eh?"

And Ah Fat would sit back and say nothing and
look nothing, while San Lee would droop her eyes
and roll her head and worship. Very powerful was
Ah Fat in Chinatown. He was the chief of his
Tong (The Silver Chrysanthemum), and men had
named him the Fire-spouting Dragon. Greed sat
upon his brow and ate into his skin. He was the
richest of all the Quarter, and his riches had come
to him by the misfortunes of others: not by the
honourable means of trade or the gaming-table.
He was a money-lender, and crafty in his method.
When sums loaned became due, he would simulate

kindly concern with the affairs of his debtor, and would gently pass back a portion of the money; and few were at first sufficiently keen-witted to detect the trick. Always he was affably ready with cash assistance to the needy and unfortunate; and as men do not freely talk of their pecuniary embarrassments, or compare notes upon their treatment by usurers, it came about that half Chinatown was in great or small degree in his power. When he began to use his power he became a nuisance; and store-keepers and laundry-men began to suffer acute disorder of mind. Unable to resist his power, they directed their animosity against those of his Tong; and again those street battles, which Boy Blue had so often quelled, broke out again. This caused so much irritation to peaceful seamen and dock workers, who found that public bloodshed interrupted their private beer-shed, that complaints were laid; and Boy Blue was assigned to see to it.

He saw to it, and, from his inquiries, learnt the full story of the iniquities of Ah Fat in the matter of his usury. He reported. Plans were then laid for breaking the power of Ah Fat and his Tong, and relieving his victims from his duress; and news of these plans came to Ah Fat.

Ah Fat set himself to see to it. He waddled about his tea-house and his kitchen, and thought. Then he sent for San Lee.

"Dissa Big Boy Blue," he said, "he get veh busy

jus' now. Big Boy Blue he make heap damn fella
trouble." He smiled and showed his teeth, pink
from much chewing of areca-nut.

San Lee listened and said nothing.

"Dissa Big Boy Blue—he gotta *go!*" And San
Lee shivered. "He gotta go—quick!"

He left her then, and went to the kitchen. In
the evening he came to her again.

"He too quick and clever for Ah Fat. He no
trust Ah Fat. He watch evehting Ah Fat do. Yoh
poh un'appy father—he got no way to mek Big
Boy Blue go. But li'l Ah San Lee—Big Boy
Blue no watch her like he watch Ah Fat. San Lee,
she 'elp 'er ole father?"

San Lee stood mute under the steady drip of his
words.

Next day he spoke again, plaintively, of the
trouble that Boy Blue's activities implied to him;
and he threw out hints to San Lee; hints that filled
her with horror and set her skin tingling with
loathing. Boy Blue was her prince—remote, inaccessible, austere, but a prince, the fact of whose
existence thrilled her with rapture. It seemed even
presumption on her part to attempt to shield so
noble a figure from danger; but she attempted. She
pondered how to give him warning, but Ah Fat
was watchful. "Huh! Huh! You like-a dissa
Big Boy Blue, huh? So!" Not a step could she
take from the kitchen; no chance came to her of

passing to the kindly Ho Ling, who had long desired her, such a message as he might convey to Boy
Blue.

That night, when she had again and flatly refused to carry out the wishes of her honourable
father, he took her to the basement beneath the
kitchen, and there, for some hours, he employed
certain terrible means of persuasion. And when
he carried her up, bruised and torn, she was pliant
to his will. He was not accustomed to being
thwarted.

"So nex' time Missa Big Boy Blue 'e come, you
know watta we do, huh?"

And San Lee implied that she understood.

Boy Blue continued his inquiries and spoke to
his colleagues of their fruit. "I shall have to have
another chat with Mr. Ah Fat. That kid of his
had been mighty useful to me, at times. He's as
cute as they make 'em, but she's like a baby. She
may know something that'll put the lid on him."

So at ten o'clock the next Saturday he went in
plain clothes to Mr. Ah Fat's tea-room. The bars
were closing, and much noise beat about the by-
ways. The rum-hounds of Limehouse bayed to the
moon. Random whiffs of chandoo came to his nose.
He made a note of the house whence they came,
and decided to see to it to-morrow; and passed
on through the heavy, dry air of the Quarter. As
he turned into Pennyfields, Ah Fat was watching

from his window. With a lumbering but swift
movement he waddled to the tea-room, seized a
rod of split bamboo, and stood over San Lee.

" 'E come. 'E come to damage yoh poh father.
You 'member what I say?"

She nodded. He looked at her doubtfully, and
brandished the bamboo; then moved swiftly to the
kitchen and made hasty preparation for the coming of Boy Blue. Then he called San Lee to the
kitchen, and pointed to a tray on which stood two
cups. He shook her and showed her the cup nearest the edge of the tray. "Dissa cup, San Lee.
Dissa cup, O affliction to a miserable father. You
savee?"

San Lee nodded with blank face, gulping and
quivering, and Ah Fat folded his hands and also
nodded. He was in no mood to put up with a re-
calcitrant child. The occasion was desperate and
called for extreme action. If Boy Blue were suc-
cessful in his plan for breaking his power, he was
wholly undone. He could no longer hold his head
high above the poor wretches of storekeepers and
laundrymen whose names stood on the wrong side
of his account leaves. He would be a figure for
ridicule. Men would doff their gravity at sight
of him. He would be abject. Life would not be
worth living. It must not happen. Anything before that. It should not happen. He was careless

of all other consequences if he could avert that supreme disaster.

As the lumbering tread of Boy Blue was heard on the stairs, he shook her again—"Dissa cup, huh?"—released her, and descended to the cellar. When Boy Blue entered the tea-room, she went forward, following, dazedly, the part that had been so sharply taught her. Even as she walked, Ah Fat seemed to be at her side, and his dreadful voice in her ear, exacting obedience to his commands under pain of sufferings worse than death. If she failed to play her part, if she warned Boy Blue of his danger, torments unbearable lay in store for her. But there was one other way of saving him —a way which she could face with even mind.

"Ho, good-ev-en-ing, sir. You wan' look around? Ho yess, sir. I so sorry Misteh Ah Fat 'e not-atome. 'E be in veh soon."

Boy Blue looked down at her and chuckled her under the chin with a large hand. "Right-o, Angel-Face. And what's the latest with you, eh? I'll come in and wait for Mr. Ah Fat." He loomed above her down the passage, his lounge suit as severe as armour in contrast to the dumpling figure in slack linen; his burly boots gigantic alongside the timid list slippers. He had his eyes all about him, and pushed open the door of the kitchen and looked round it. He saw nothing to disturb him, and followed San Lee to the table near the window. She

did not give him the smiles and head-wagging which
usually greeted his persiflage, but he paid no heed
to it, beyond remarking: "What's up, kiddie? Got
the fantoodleums?"

"Ho no, misteh. I veh tired. You like li'l suey
sen, sir? You take cuppa tea with me?"

"Tea? Well, I don't mind if I do. A slice o'
lemon in mine. Then if you shut the door we can
have a quiet li'l talk, eh?"

"Ollight. I go get tea."

She went into the kitchen and got the tray, and
got a glowering look from the face of Ah Fat,
which was level with the top of the cellar stairs. She
returned to the tea-room, carrying the tray with
nice care. She set it down and looked behind her
to the kitchen. From the street came throbs of
dark sound, above which climbed the lugubrious
wail of a fiddle and the grinding of a gramophone.
She stood stolid at the table. Her great moment
had come. Her hero was in danger of his life, and
must at all cost be saved. She alone—sweet thought
—could save him. The cellar beneath the kitchen
had in its time held many secrets, but it should not
hold Boy Blue. It was rapture for her, this moment that had given to her the chance of rendering
to him the highest of all service. Covering the
tray with her person, she took a piece of lemon
from a plate and dropped it in the cup that stood

in the middle of the tray; and passed the cup steadily to her guest.

The other cup she took herself, and sat down opposite Boy Blue.

"We dlink together, sir. As yoh gentlemen say: I look towahds you. And veh soon I tell you something useful."

"Well, cheerio, kid."

They drank. San Lee sat calm, her eyes fixed on Boy Blue. He noted the steady gaze, and, knowing the Chinks, let her take her own time for disclosing what she had to disclose. But she was only trying to tell him through her eyes that she was glad, and that in a moment he would have a clear case against Ah Fat. She took another mouthful from the cup, and felt free to speak, for she knew that she was going beyond the reach of any human persecution. But when she opened her mouth she found she could not speak. No matter. Boy Blue would soon discover the truth for himself.

As she felt the sudden sharp pains stabbing her limbs, and the cold damp upon her face, happiness beyond words was hers. She had given all that she had to give to her valiant prince, and great was the joy of giving. Her head drooped, for it was very heavy; but she felt that his eyes were upon her, and felt them as a parting benediction, a *Nunc dimittis.*

Until, with an effort, she raised her head to meet his glance, and saw his face. In his eyes was a look

of awful questioning. His face was as marble-
white as hers. Sweat stood in beads upon his skin.
As the room glimmered about her and the walls
approached and receded, the last look that she received from her hero was one of unutterable and un-
quenchable hatred. Ere he collapsed, he seized the
cup he had received from her hands and flung it full
at her.

Ah Fat, being no sport, and taking no chance with
undutiful daughters, had poisoned both cups.

MAZURKA

— XII —

MAZURKA

CHRISSIE RAINBOW stood on the balcony of her tenement home and looked down upon the evening life of Limehouse. In the warm sapphire dusk even the vociferant dock-side lay hushed, expectant; and footsteps crackled like fireworks. Clusters of boys and girls hung at street corners, chatting and softly giggling. Yellow men paired with silent, ogling females, and swam into quiet by-ways. Hard-faced women collared simple sailors. Malays hovered and desired, not daring to pounce.

Then the big lamp outside the Blue Lantern was lit, and lights appeared behind its many windows, and an organ stopped at its doors, and sprayed the neighbourhood with a rapid fire of rag-time. Its bright summons set young feet a-tapping and old heads a-wagging, and into the gas-lit circle moved flaring hats and wide-grinning faces. The great sea of roofs that swept out to Essex began to twinkle with luminous points, and all-night factories made gashes of light across the distant gloom.

As the twilight deepened to night the loungers began to pull themselves together and to make certain movements towards substantial entertainment.
The two music halls, shrinking behind their bold
veils of light, flung open their doors to a clamant
crowd of seekers after mirth. The cinemas were
"now showing," vehemently, Lillian Gish and
Nazimova.

The organ stopped its ragging. Chrissie heard
its rasping wheels bear it away, and with its passing the motley murmur of the crowd again vexed her
ears with its uneasy calm. For some minutes she
stood thus, drawing to herself the breath of the
city. Then from the little Chinese café at the
corner of King's Street came a sudden burst of music,
as its latest attraction, a penny-in-the-slot piano,
clattered its way through a new record—the
Mazurka from *Coppèlia*.

Straight through the open window to her it came,
riding joyously, insolently, above the purring street;
and it captured the idle half of her mind, and she
found herself smiling in welcome to it! The chorus
songs of the street she knew, and the organ music
which had just passed; and felt at no time any
litheness of limb to their rhythms. But here was
something novel; charged with colour and various
melody, and rippling with lightness of heart and
holiday; something strange to her, yet made to her
own heart's measure. It carried to her an invitation

as flagrant as the nod and beck of a passing reveller
at carnival. It disturbed her and set her in effer-
vescence. The tired, purposeless crowd below took
on colour for her eyes; she saw them at revels.
And while the saucy, provocative phrases of the
Mazurka stirred her heart to petulance, her skin
tingled with delight, vibrating to them.

And, suddenly, she wanted to be out—just Out:
anywhere with the crowd, touching fingers or brush-
ing shoulders with people; looking into other faces,
and mixing and exchanging emotions. It teased
her with its message. She wanted to throw herself
into this London and become one with it and part
of it. Like a caged bird she stood, her breast against
the bars of the balcony, her arms outstretched to
the great plain of London. Blunt of face, and
without colour, she yet held charm in her figure.
Sturdy and pliant as a young tree she stood, her
frock blown, her limbs rippling to the music, her
face rapt. Twice the mechanical contraption went
through the new record, while she stood and longed
and bubbled with foolish smiles.

With an impudently triumphant flourish it finished, and she turned slowly away to her room.
In the chill halfgloom of the summer night, it
looked mean and fusty and bare. She discovered
a sudden disgust of it and its petty appointments.
She moved about it. She picked up a book, and
threw it down. She sat on the edge of the bed.

She got up and straightened an ornament on the mantelshelf. She again took up the book. But her mind was outside. She was listening to the crisp gossip of young feet to the pavement. She was seeing the long Barking Road—all breeze and glare and glitter of lamps and shop windows. She was seeing the happy encounters of boy and girl; and she *felt* the odour of lilac floating from the public gardens. The streets were breathing softly, closely, wooing her. The Mazurka still simmered within her.

Until to-night her evenings had followed a changeless routine. Home from the factory—wash —a meal of some tinned food and tea—necessary repairs to garments—then a book of some educational course—and bed. By her fellows at the factory she was voted slow. Miss Stuck-up was her name there. "Look at The Stuck-up going 'ome to keep 'erself *Pure!*" "We ain't good enough for the chaste Stuck-up!" All their invitations to "evenings" and "crawls," to " 'ave a bit on," she declined; and when, on the pavement outside the factory, the girls stood in chattering groups, to argue the evening's indulgence, she would slip through them and away, followed by muttered obscenities. To all their gibes she had one reply— an exasperating smile of self-sufficiency.

But to-night she could not rest; she was not company for herself. The benignant dusk, the crooning of the summer evening, and the bright challenge of the Mazurka had entered her blood. Solitude now distressed her. She longed to be in the life that was all about her. She longed to be accepted by the crowd, and to be one of it; and suddenly she rose from the bed, snatched her hat, and adjusted it at a rakish angle. With a few deft touches she smoothed the poor cotton frock; then, with thrilling pulses, she ran down the stone stairs to the street, and surrendered herself to the crowd.

She was Out. Cleverly she copied the saunter of the other girls: the swinging arms, the swirling frock, the roving eye. In the high charm of her fifteen years she strode. Her thin brown hair flowed about her shoulders, and the swift lines of her limber legs curved aptly from pendulous skirt to natty shoe. She was prepared now to accept all things, and to find greater joy in the common street. She needed not to-night the rarefied atmosphere in which she had hitherto held herself from contact with the mob. She had come down off her perch, and was now warm and fluent.

But the street made no demonstration at her condescension. None looked twice at her. The East End boy looks only for faces; if they be not pretty, all other charms are without virtue. She searched here and there for some of her work-fellows. They were certainly "out," amusing themselves somewhere, and it would be pleasant to join them. It would be pleasant to be popular with them. They would perhaps find her a boy, who would walk with her and take her arm; for she thought that she wanted a boy to walk out with and talk with. Really, she wanted to talk with London and be friends with it.

Up and down the street she strolled, but saw no familiar face, nor any that sought to make itself known. Tiring after four turns, she went to the Tunnel Gardens; and here she boldly invited with feet and eyes. A few lads looked at her, but with sniggers and ribald comment. These were the knowing ones, who chose carefully. "Pasty-face!" was the welcome she got from them. Other lads looked at her without remark, but these were the bashful, the inexperienced, who did not know how to force an introduction; novices, like herself.

But at the farther gate of the Gardens she found Adventure. Mr. Sam Ling Lee, in straw hat, brown boots and store suit, was leaning against a railing, twirling a whangee cane. His face was placid, his appearance highly respectable; and he seemed lonely. She came to him and passed him with a flutter of frock, and gave him a long, expressive look. He smiled. Some paces away, she looked back. He was still looking. She stopped at the railings, and smiled. He came to her.

Well, they walked out of the gardens towards Pennyfields. Great elation was hers, and her little

lips were pursed tightly to hold back the smile that
would have lodged there. She was living. She
had Got Off. She was no longer to be sneered at
as the Stuck-up, the timid. She could cut a dash
as well as anyone else. Mr. Sam Ling Lee, too,
was proud. A white girl had given him the glad eye,
and was coming to Pennyfields to take a cup of
tohah and to eat with him.

At the tea-house of the Golden Chrysanthemum
they sat at a marble table; and she drank tea and
ate little cakes, and thrilled to his quaint accent
the turns of speech. And he leaned across the
table and pressed her hand, and she returned the
squeeze. And he told her, by many difficult words,
that he knew the keeper of the tea-house, and that
there was a nice quiet room upstairs where they
could sit and talk. And he would like to sit and talk
with her.

So they went upstairs.

It was past public-house closing-time when she
came down. She stepped into Pennyfields, narrow,
dark and deserted, and her light shoes made clear
staccato sounds. She walked dreamily. Her eyes
were heavy. But there was a warmth and fullness
about her face that was new, and that became her.
She carried herself with confidence. She was a
woman. The others could no longer swank before
her. She knew.

Then, as she turned into West India Dock

Road, the darkness screamed at her. Snarls and growls and cat-calls met her, and vile words leapt upon her. And suddenly she was surrounded by a dozen of her work-fellows. Too dazed by the attack to speak, she shrank away. But they were on all sides: horrid faces and writhing lips that spat beastly things at her. The full significance of the situation scarcely reached her at the moment. It was an attack; that was all she could clearly understand; and she turned blindly to break through them and run. And as she turned, one pushed her between the shoulders, and she stumbled against another who pushed her back. Dumb, except for sobs, she waited, terrified, in their midst; and they encircled her with stretched arms and pointed fingers; and she stood breasting a ring of living spears.

Then they joined hands, and danced about her with a song:

> "Who got orf with a Chink?
> Who got orf with a Chink?
> She did!
> *She did!*
> SHE DID!
>   Yah!"

And from point to point of the circle she was pushed and hustled and bunted like a sack, until she dropped.

Then, clamorously, they indicted her: "There's

yer quiet ones! There's yer pure work-girl. There's yer Stuck-up! Gorn with a Chink! Ugh, the dirty cat! That's all that would 'ave 'er, I suppose. Ugh, the dirty bitch!" They let her go then, and went off in a grinning, giggling mass, chanting to the night:

"Chrissie Rainbow's bin with a Chink
Yah! Yah! Yah!"

Slowly she crawled to her feet, and slowly she crawled home, numb, sobbing, stricken. It was spring no more. The scent of flowers was gone. The air was heavy with the religious odour of fried fish. There was no more of colour and revelry and happy street life. She looked upon the every-night Limehouse, and saw grey streets, gruff buildings, ragged roofs and walls, tram-cars, buses, dark pubs, and ugly, dolorous noise. And as she staggered into her room, and collapsed upon her bed, an uglier noise broke forth below, and a damned jingling, hiccuping, penny-in-the-slot piano gibed and reviled her with the Mazurka from *Coppèlia*.

THE SCARLET SHOES

— XIII —

THE SCARLET SHOES

SORROWFUL are the streets of Limehouse by
day; crowded with purposeless noise and cold,
unfruitful endeavour. But the evening is kind to
them, and with the coming of the dark they are set
a-tinkling with brilliant girl-laughter, and the moon
lends grace to the most forlorn by-way.

About these streets and lanes walked one time
San-li-po, a maiden of the land of water-liles, whose
patched garments of yellow cotton, with cheap em-
broidery enriched, gave vigour to the flat tones of
warehouse walls and hovels. Willowy and dew-
like was San-li-po, but seldom did her laughter swell
the happy twilight chorus. Not since babyhood
had her lips opened in merriment, for there was
little in her life to warm her heart to satisfaction.
A waif, born in the Pool on an incoming tramp,
and abandoned to the clustering alleys, she had
found her first shelter with the wicked Lee Yip, and
with him, because she was in a strange land and
knew of no other shelter, she had remained these
seventeen years. Hard and cheerless was her life
with him; nor could the animated streets give her

even a reflection of their gladness. The white men mocked at her moon-like face; her countrymen regarded her not while they might feed their eyes with the beauty of white girls.

Lee Yip was a man of low mind and empty of all good feeling. All he desired was sufficiency of rice-spirit and ongaway, and, despite all his forlorn shifts and subterfuges, never could he fully satisfy that desire. His nights were spent in drinking; his days in petulant consideration of ways and means of procuring the night's indulgence. Dirt and rags were proper to him, and he seemed to shed their savour wherever he walked; so that refined and polished keepers of stores and of registered lodging-houses, coming suddenly upon him, would pass him with as much space between them as could be achieved. One room he had over the Laundry of the Pure White Water-Lily; and in that room lived he and San-li-po. To it he would sometimes bring stranded Chinese seamen of the baser kind, who would not pay the price of the registered lodging-houses, but could give him, in return for his shelter, the few cash that would buy rice-spirit; and San-li-po would crouch unhappily upon her pallet in the corner, and sleep fearfully in this room with four or five drunken seamen.

But it is with one night in winter that we are here concerned; the night when sweet adventure came to his sad room and stretched radiant hands

towards San-li-po. At a late hour on this night,
Lee Yip made his accustomed entry to their abode,
fumbling and shouldering his way up the stairs, and
emitting nasty noises from his mouth. San-li-po,
hearing other footsteps yet on the stairs, stood by
the table with blank expression, ready to receive
the wretched fellows who alone would consort with
her guardian.

And lo! there entered to her Wing Dee, a youth
of fair aspect and seemly demeanour. His hair
was heavily oiled. His eyes were reticent. He
held himself upright in his canvas jacket and canvas
trousers, and when he perceived San-li-po, his round
face glowed like a lit lantern. He did not slouch
to a corner, with pig-like sounds, as their other
guests: he passed compliments to her; asked if she
had eaten her rice; and continued, using a courteous
form of phrase above the requirements of the occasion:

"This person is mortified at the inconvenience
which he fears his undignified presence in this truly
refined apartment will bring upon the honourable
and flower-like maiden to whom he addresses himself. He would not have ventured, but——"

He was interrupted at this point by Lee Yip,
who had spoken no word since his entrance, because he could not. With a gentle sway he slid
along the wall against which he had been leaning,
and fell in an untidy heap to the floor and slept.

Wing Dee looked at him and at San-li-po, and trouble came into his face; then, ignoring the interruption, he continued his courteous address. Now these wer: the first polished words that any visitor had addressed to San-li-po, and she shivered with delight as she heard them, while wondering grievously whether the apparently gentle youth was subjecting her to ridicule. But as he continued to speak, she knew that this was not so, and her heart leapt; and she hastened to prepare food for the honourable guest.

With Lee Yip in his drunken sleep, they were virtually alone, this man and this maid, and much joyful service did she give to the making of that poor meal which they were to share; the cook of the highest mandarin could not have pressed more care upon a banquet of forty courses than she on two dishes of yak min and sam se. The eyes of Wing Dee were upon her as she worked, and now and then she caught them with hers, and into the dishes went a sweet flavouring that was made from the mixing of their glances.

When her task was done, they two sat to eat in bashful intimacy; and while Lee Yip snored on the floor, Wing Dee made neat praise of the dishes, and smiled upon the lips of San-li-po that made their first shy efforts at opening in delight. Sweet lips that never formed a lie; that moved only to gentle syllables and pleading phrases! Grave eyes wherein nestled meditations pure and kindly! Gracious hands, busy only in service to the beast in the corner! Poor, tattered clothes, so thin and worn, yet clothing so aptly that small figure that should have gone in silk and lace! Thoughts of the Great Night Lantern above fair gardens came to Wing Dee as he gazed his fill upon her until she burned and shivered and looked only at the table, and as he wondered about her and about the room and the pig who had brought him here; and his face became suffused with the divine humility that at once shames and ennobles the youth in the presence of his first maid. She spoke little to him save single timid words in reply to his compliments; but something more potent than words passed between them.

After the meal, she pointed to a corner, and to it he retired and she went to her pallet. Sleep came at once to her, and with it gracious adventures with a fair and high-minded youth; but Wing Dee lay awake through the long night and the velvet voice of silence murmured from the darkness and spoke beautiful words to him. He thought of his own country; of rivers; of stars; of blossomtime; of a goodly house with many servants, and of San-li-po in costly raiment flitting about it. Then the grey of the morning fell across the coloured dream, and he hid it away in his heart. He awoke to the rough room, and Lee Yip's beastly noise. He rose from the chill boards and looked out upon the sunless street and its fatigued activity. He looked at the sodden face of Lee Yip, and shuddered. Towards the corner where lay San-li-po his heart forbade him to look, though great was his desire to go to her, and place by her pallet goodly gifts of warm silk. But he knew that he had scarce sufficient money to procure food for the space of days that must elapse before the ship that had engaged him left London. Even the poorest offering was beyond him, for a chance game of Peh Bin had cleared him of the bulk of his wages, and it was in that impoverished and remorseful condition that Lee Yip had found him.

Suddenly, at a movement and a grunt from Lee Yop, San-li-po awoke. Hastily gathering her robe about her, she exchanged morning greetings with Wing Dee, and served out a small portion of rice to each of them. When it was eaten he turned to go. He passed to the mumbling and still bemused Lee Yip the number of coins previously arranged between them as the price of his lodging, and moved to the door. He made a gesture of courtesy towards San-li-po.

"This illiterate person," he said, "is totally without words with which to express his intense gratitude for the refined and elegant entertainment which he has received from his dignified and high-minded friends."

He hesitated at the door. He looked back. And lo! San-li-po was staring at him with rigid features and blank eyes. Maiden modesty was no longer in her bearing: her face spoke yearning and regret.

She knew nothing of him, nor he of her. He had come to them out of the night. He had looked long upon her, and had spoken fair words to her. But that was all. Whence he came, whither he was going, she knew not; nor could she decently ask of him these questions. His movements were no concern of hers. Doubtless he had spoken courteously and kindly towards her, because he was sorry for her situation. Yet, having had this little of him, she was anxious that he should give more.

"Honourable guest going—going away?" she murmured, and stopped with half-open lips, as though about to say more.

Wing Dee caught the restrained fervour of her voice, and rejoiced that she should thus have spoken. So would he have spoken his regret at parting; yet dared not.

"If this insignificant person might come again to-night——" he began, looking at her and Lee Yip.

Lee Yip nodded his tattered head vigorously. "Come every night," he grunted. "For the few cash which this person charges for his lodging, poor as it is, Wing Dee cannot find better. Ao!"

So he came again that night, and, after leaving
the house the following morning, he met San-li-po
in the streets. There, at a corner of West India
Dock Road, they talked. They told each other their
stories. With awkward glances and shy hesitancies,
with gushes of speech and cold blocks of silence,
they exchanged talk for about an hour, each de-
lighting in this sudden meeting, each fearful of
saying too much. They parted abruptly, rudely, as
is the way of boy and girl in first love. But when
they were gone on their way, they knew that each
was the other's friend for ever, and great was the
desire of Wing Dee to lift San-li-po across his
threshold; great the desire of San-li-po to receive
the Napi of Wing Dee.

Four nights he spent as their lodger; and joy
illumined that musty room, and sweetness passed
in the air and hovered about the table as they sat
at rice. All things became beautiful to him. He
found delight in the narrow alley where she lived;
and its stones were to him more holy than the stones
of the temple. These strange streets were all part
of her, and she was part of the streets and the
hard sky and the ships; and the mean life of Chinatown became to him suddenly noble and desirable:
for it was the life she knew. His immediate wish
was to remove her from the beast in whose charge
she was held, but the wish, he knew, was futile.
Hatred and loathing seethed in his heart as he

thought upon the things that the maid had told him, and he longed again to lay violent fingers upon the wry neck of Lee Yip.

At the end of the week, much thought showed him the way to his desire. He would not rejoin his ship. He would stay in Limehouse and work at any toil, however base, until he had saved enough money to carry them both to his own country. There they would marry, and he would settle on his father's farm and work it for her delight. To this plan he moved, and, after some disappointment and much perseverance, he obtained employment, and employment in the Laundry of the Pure Water-White Lily, above which she lived. By sparse living and a little fortunate gambling, he contrived to gather and hold a few coins; then, delicate of feeling, he slept no more in her room, but obtained lodging in a neighbouring Oriental store where he might still be near her, and in any mischance, succor her.

Each night, when his work was done, and the fat Lee Yip had gone forth to seek delight in the saloons and beer-houses about the waterside, he would go to San-li-po, and they would spend together some delicious hours.

"O San-li-po, your voice is to me as the bells of the Great Temple, and you are a garden where I gather the most dignified rest and refreshment. Soon, O San-li-po, I shall take you home to your country that you have never seen, and there by my side you will taste pleasures of which you have never learnt."

"O Wing Dee, lord and master, your words are more intoxicating to me than the most rare perfumes. I am your slave."

As the hour grew late, he would leave her, and wait in the West India Dock Road for the homecoming of her drunken protector. When he saw him bringing other drunkards to sleep in that room with his chrysanthemum, he would approach the sailors stealthily, and draw them apart from their staggering guide; and would put it to them whether it were not entirely more desirable that they should spend the night in his clean room without charge than that they should pay valuable coins to the drunken Lee Yip for the privilege of sleeping in the underground den infested with rats and drain-water, to which he was conducting them. By his knowledge and use of sailor signs he was quickly able to convince them of evil reputation of Lee Yip. So that this person, arriving at the door leading to his room, would be seized by vague astonishment and sharp anger on finding that the guests who had been following him had melted away; and San-li-po, waiting upstairs, would be rid of her disquieting tremors, and, smiling at her lover's ruse, would sleep tranquilly.

Now it was not long before Wing Dee possessed

sufficient cash to permit him to make his first gift
of intentions to San-li-po. After much scrutiny of
shop windows, he saw something that was within
his means and fitting to the occasion. At a shop
near Limehouse Church his eye was taken by a hot
splash of colour—a pair of slippers of scarlet silk,
made surely for the dainty feet of his maid. Long
he looked upon them, while delicious thrills tickled
his heart. They were to be the first gift he had
ever made to a girl, and they were to symbolise
his worship of little San-li-po, and set a glowing
seal upon their friendship. He looked upon the
warm, suave silk that sheathed them, and the little
pert bows that embellished them, and saw them
upon her feet, peeping from the patched cotton
robe, and thought how they would chime with and
confirm her olive face and golden eyes. Then, with
happy assurance, he entered the shop and cere-
moniously paid the price that should secure them.
Close to his heart he held them as he walked home,
and they seemed to pass through the canvas of his
coat and glow against his breast and lend him
warmth.

That evening, when they were alone, he made
his offering. He took them from the rough paper
in which they were wrapped, and standing before
her, he covered them with kisses and breathed his
sweet heart into him. Then, while she trilled de-
lightedly to him, he placed them tenderly upon her

feet. Immediately she arose and pirouetted before him, and pattered up and down the bare floor of her home, and could look only from the shoes to her lover and from her lover to the shoes; until at last she tripped into the half-circle of his arms and he knew that glory had been vouchsafed him. Gladly she came to him, and sweetly danced the hours of that evening around them.

Now vigorously and sturdily he worked in the laundry, urged by the imperious patter of little scarlet feet on the floor above him, tapping out messages of behest and encouragement. None moved about so spryly as he. None washed and starched with such industry and such accompaniment of smiles and polished address. The lamp of his soul which he had long kept so neatly trimmed was now lighted by love, and shone through his blunt face for all to see. So life went fairly for them for many days.

Then trouble came. One midnight, as he watched near the poor temple of his lady, Lee Yip approached, and with him were three dishevelled water-rats. Lee Yip was drunk, and reeled; turning now and again to beckon his guests to follow him, and reeling at every turn. Swiftly Wing Dee noted the situation; and as they drew near he slipped from his hiding place and crept between host and guests. Turning to the seamen, he muttered a seaman's greeting, gave them a sign of warning, and hustled them into an alley-way. There he told them, with prodigal embellishment of fact, of the offensive hovel to which Lee Yip was taking them, and made them his accustomed offer of free accommodation in his own room. Some interchange of talk convinced the seamen that the offer was of fair intent, and that Wing Dee was one topside good fella chap; and the four went from the alley by the farther outlet.

But Lee Yip, drunk as he was, retained yet some control of his faculties. Too often lately had evil spirits, hovering in the middle air, swooped down and removed from his custody likely guests from whom good measures of rice-spirit might have been obtained; and when he discovered that this evening's company had also vanished, he felt that the time had come to turn his mind upon the matter. Calling upon his ancestors, he slithered across the road, looked at the doors about him, and found them shut; and up and down the street, and found it empty. He came to the mouth of the alley, and looked down it, and he was there in time to see four dim figures disappearing at the other end. Towards them he shuffled at an angular run, and came stealthily to them. With well-nigh insufferable indignation he recognised his guests, and heard the voice of Wing Dee conversing affably with them on the base reputation and horrid iniquities of himself, Lee Yip.

In a state of amazement and disgust he retired
abruptly to the shelter of the alley, and crouched
against the wall. The sudden shock of this discovery drove the drink swiftly from his brain, and
left his faculties clear, though its poison still turned
and crawled in his blood. He reviewed the situation
in detail. He saw himself outraged, scoffed at, reviled behind his back by this pig of a seaman who
had eaten of his rice. Seeking a motive, he suddenly remembered San-li-po, and here he saw clearly
things that his bemused mind had noted without
fully perceiving their import. He began to remember certain looks that had passed between San-li-po
and Wing Dee in his room at evenings. He began
to remember that the meals that San-li-po had cooked
when the youth was present were more sumptuous
and more daintily served than those to which he
had accustomed him. He remembered now, very
sharply, how San-li-po had often served larger por-
tions and choicer tit-bits to the guest than to himself.

And now two streams of anger broke from his
breast and surged through him: one against the
youth; the other, the greater, against the outcast
waif, San-li-po, who had thus basely deceived him
by accepting the advances of this pig who sought
to rob him of his means of life. Hot was his rage
against the base and treacherous thing that had
subsisted on his charity these many years, when no
other would help her, and now had turned against

him. He could not conjecture why these two should wish to do him harm; he only saw himself as the victim of their malicious hearts; and sorely upbraided himself for showing kindness to a woman.

Then the two streams of anger united, and became one, and in their murky waters a dreadful dark thing began to grow. He faced the way that Wing Dee had gone, and made cruel signs with his hand, and his mouth bristled with vile words; and his brain fed on the dark things and gave back sustenance to it. By the time he reached his door the thing had grown until it had full possession of him; and he stumbled up the stairs to work his wrath upon the corrupt deceiver whom he had so long harboured in his home, and, through her, upon the guest who had abused his roof.

When he entered, San-li-po was sitting on the floor, and from her towzled skirt peeped the little scarlet shoes which were tapping the floor to some secret tune of glee. His dull eye sharply noted them, for she had not yet worn them in his presence, and he guessed whence they came; and the flood of his anger threatened to break its gates. He controlled himself. With deliberate thickness of speech and with heavy countenance he approached her.

"O San-li-po, there is one asking for you. He desires to speak at once with you. It is the young guest who lately visited our dwelling. He is at the tea-house of Ho Foo in some distress. There

was a base and undignified disturbance at the Blue
Lantern, and he lies wounded. I think his mind
wanders and he speaks from the middle air, for he
spoke much of you and requested me to bring you
to him."

Sore alarm rose to the quiet eyes of San-li-po
at these words, and Lee Yip noted it, and knew
then that she was indeed in conspiracy with that
person against him. She moved quickly to a peg
where hung a loose covering robe. This she
wrapped about her, and they went out to the dark
streets and into the flowing hum of London's silence.
Through road and alley they went, he lumbering in
his broken British boots, she in the scarlet shoes
that tripped along with her to the sick one who had
given them. They passed from the Causeway to
Narrow Street, and so under many arches that held
uncomfortable noises.

"Did I mistake, O Sun at Noon? I thought you
spoke of the tea-house of Ho Foo, which is in——"

Lee Yip replied with a snarl and a grunt; and,
lest she offend him at this time when her presence
was so much desired by another, she kept silence
and followed him. Down a sloping lane of coal-
dust he led her, till, at a sudden turn, they faced
the broad, rough river. Behind them were the
arches; on either side deserted wharves. Then he
turned upon her.

"O San-li-po, creature of corruption and deceit!

O venomous snake! O female dog of the city! O pig of behaviour! Your insufferable conspiracy against the one who has fed you and clothed you is known to me. The nature of your relations with the detestable and evil-minded Wing Dee is known to me. It is for some purpose which you know that he takes from me my evening guests, my only means of living. It is because of you that he has taken to labour in the clothes-cleansing business below our apartment. What more is in your black heart I know not, but never shall it come out to injure me. Hi-yah!"

Ere she could utter one word or cry he fell upon her. With his curling hands he worked for some minutes what beastliness he would upon her. Then he took her by the throat, tore from her her garments, lifted her from the ground, and dropped her from the wharf to the full, surging river; and the waters closed upon her.

Next morning, as Wing Dee plunged a mass of clothes into the boiling cauldron, and worked vigorously upon them, he listened for his morning greeting—the patter of little shoes upon the floor above —and was disappointed that he did not hear it. He continued his work with quickened ears, awaiting it, but throughout the morning no sound came from that upper room. He was disturbed; and at midday he went upstairs to see. Neither Lee Yip nor San-li-po was there. He worked automatically through the afternoon without zest, wondering at this interruption of habit, and fearing and dismissing fear. In the evening he went again to the room. It was still vacant. He inquired of people about the street for San-li-po, but none could answer him. He sought the saloons of the Quarter for Lee Yip, but found him not, nor had any seen him or had word of him. When shops, teahouses and saloons all were closed, he returned to his room in a spirit of no-tranquillity. There he bowed before the joss, and lit a joss-stick, and burned prayer papers; but no comfort came to him, and the night passed with hollow tread. Empty of hope, too, was the next day. There was no sign or sound of San-li-po, and as he worked in the laundry with languid arms, his mind moved upon their happy times together. Again he went to the room, and found it still deserted, and though he sought he found no poor robe of hers nor the scarlet shoes. She was gone, fully dressed. Now grief and dismay entered his heart and settled there; and in the evening he went to his room, and stood against its wall, empty of purpose and with no appetite for sleep. His mind wandered, and as it wandered about their love, he remembered how, when he had presented his gift of intentions, the scarlet shoes, he had bestowed his kisses upon them and breathed into them, that they should be for ever part of him, and that San-li-po should ever have something of him about her.

And remembering this, he called softly upon them:

"O little scarlet shoes that I placed upon the feet of the willowy and dew-like San-li-po, if you are with her bring her to me. Little shoes, you are part of me, for I left myself inside you when I gave you to her. Come to me, O little scarlet shoes. Carry her to me or bring me news of her."

And he bowed his head to the wall, and stood thus, while the hours crept across the face of the night. Suddenly, when the mid-hour had newly passed, he seemed to hear, through the enveloping quiet, a gentle clatter as of little feet on the pavement. With leaping heart he looked from his window. The street was dark and void of any human figure, and no sound came up from its shadow. He turned away, and his arms dropped in dolour. But again he heard it, and this time it was a distinct sound of feet on his stair. He stood still and tense, listening. The sound drew nearer, and now pattered outside his door—it seemed to him, impatiently, pleadingly.

With vague tremblings in his breast, he stole softly to the door, stretched a hesitating hand to the fastening, unlatched it, and looked out. The tiny landing was empty. His hand groped at the darkness and touched nothing, and he knew that he was deceived again. But as he moved to close the door, the silence of the stairway was shattered by a peremptory stamp of little feet on the landing.

He bent close to the floor, and saw nothing, but very
clearly he heard the steps beating out their morning
message—now on the landing, now two or three
steps down, now back to the landing.

Crushing down the hope that grew within him,
he went into his room, saluted the joss, called upon
his ancestors, and returned to the doorway. Down
the stairs ran the sharp tattoo of shoes. At the
bottom they stopped. Slowly he followed them, and
opened the lower door. As he stepped into the
street, he heard them tapping the pavement that led
to West India Dock Road, and knew that this time
he was not deceived; and now in full faith he committed himself to their direction and followed them,
caring not whither they led him, confident that they
would lead him to San-li-po. Across the road they
went towards the Causeway, and above the sirens
and the clamour of the dock trains his ears picked
out their chattering guidance.

As he followed them he babbled to them, crying:

"O little scarlet shoes that have trotted so softly
beside my noisy feet, thank you for answering my
call. You are leading me to her to whom you be-
long, and soon you will be warmed again by her
little feet. I hear you singing to me, little shoes,
and I will kiss you as I kissed you before, when we
are with her."

Clitter-clatter, clitter-clatter, they tripped before
him. Lightly they kissed the pavement of that

Causeway upon whose face so many brute feet had stamped and stumbled; and the pavement was responsive to their timid touch, and whispered to them. And so they moved before him into Narrow Street, and from Narrow Street to a sloping lane of coal-dust, where he found himself on a wharf facing the river, and thence along a dark landing-stage. The sky was clouded; few stars were visible, and the river lacked even that dull lustre thrown up at night by large waters. Groping his way, he followed the steps to a narrow ledge. Here they ceased, and he halted in uncertainty. For some seconds he stood, peering into woolly darkness, listening intently for the sound of shoes. Then he took a step forward.

And so Wing Dee came to San-li-po. The tide was at flood and the waters rushed to receive him as he fell. They sucked him down and beat over him, and washed him to mid-stream, and there they came together.

.   .   .   .

Next morning there was trouble in the shop of a second-hand wardrobe dealer of Poplar.

"Hi!" cried the wife, "what about them Chinese shoes you brought 'ome the other night, what you bought orf the Chink? 'Ow much d'you give for 'em?"

"One-and-six. What about it?"

"What about it? Why, they ain't worth tuppence. They're all worn out and fit fer nothing."

"Worn out be blowed! Why, they're as good as new. They ain't bin worn more'n once. I reckon I know me own job."

"And I reckon I know what I see. The soles is worn right through, and they're smothered all over in mud. Come an' 'ave a look."

Husband came and had a look.

"Well I'm damned!"

"Huh! Good as new, eh? That's the kind o' thing you buy after a night at yer precious Blue Lantern."

"Well, I could 'a sworn——"

"Grrr!"

And the scarlet shoes, that brought two lovers together, still make domestic discord in Poplar.

THE GOOD SAMARITANS

XIV

THE GOOD SAMARITANS

IF you approach the West India Dock by way of
Commercial Road, you will notice, west of
Limehouse Church, a long, narrow street of small
houses debouching on to the highway. It is flat,
colourless, empty, by day; and by night dark and
adumbrating queer adventure. It is the street that
my memory first evokes when I think of the East
End, for it held forward place in my childish fancies.
The corner of that street I would then figure as
my meeting-place with a girl; a girl of my own
creation. We would meet at nights at that dark
corner, and from it we would survey the great road,
its bronze gloom broken by gouts of gas-light, while
behind us waited the long ranks of silent houses,
threatening and alluring, behind whose windows
happened nightly things dreadful and things beautiful. I did not make a paradise of that street, but
I gave it magic properties, and peopled it with
my own characters, so that, as occasion called, it was
a street of romance or squalor. And every night,
at its corner, stood the dream-child, waiting for

me. Sometimes she had curls of yellow, and sometimes thick black curls, or tresses of brown; and
her frocks would change from filmy things to furry,
with the season.

I have since shown my street to other people, and
they have seen a hopeless, littered alley, housing
aims without hope and hearts that have never beat
high in grace or villainy. It is to-day as it always
was. It has not grown; it has not aged; for it has
spent nothing in endeavour or desire. It is now
a street like all other streets, and holds no more
the power to change its aspect or its character. It
is no longer wholly awful or wholly romantic. No
rare adventure and gallant rescue make it their
setting. And no dream-child now stands at its
corner. Women stand there all day and through
much of the night, between the opening and the
closing times of the Blue Lantern; but my girl
went with its vanished past. The street I had
built from its ugly bricks, and the child I had placed
there could not survive inspection under the cold
light of common sense.

To-day Greenstockings and Flash Florrie, two
of the most prominent of the Blue Lantern noctam-
bulists, live in that street; and I am still foolish
enough to cherish my fancies and to believe that
they have gobbled up my dream-child. For in each
of them is something of the grace and fluent good-

ness that clothed the little girl who stood so often
at that corner.

Anyway, I now connect the street with them.
They lived together, sharing two rooms in one of
the crestfallen houses of the street; and they were
seldom without company. They kept themselves
decently, and chose their men carefully. Greenstockings was of pocket size, slender, dark, frail;
while Flash Florrie walked with masculine stride,
from wide hips, and held a large head upright under
a mass of yellow hair. She could, and sometimes
did, lift Greenstockings from the floor with one
hand. A strangely assorted couple, drawn towards
each other. They were friendly, in a casual, man-
like way, for the greater part of the year; but at
recurrent periods the lacerated nerves of Greenstockings would meet the fever-heat temper of Flash
Florrie; and then there were ructions.

Upon a night they sat together in the Blue Lantern. The hours were mounting, and the crowd
had thinned; only a few niggers and a somnolent
sailor remained. Flash Florrie had undergone
severe ordeal by bottle, and her manner gave warning of trouble. The somnolent sailor failed to
respond to her amicable approaches, and she began
to look round for something to swear at. Among
the most prized of the appointments of the Blue
Lantern are four canaries, whose cage hangs from
the chandelier above the centre of the saloon. For

many years they have lived there, syncopating, with
their piercing cries, the sedate confabulations of
bookmakers and love-bargainers, who have often
expressed the pious wish that some hungry genera-
tion would tread them down. Flash Florrie, finding her one-sided conversation with the sailor non-
productive in the way of business, turned her attention to the birds. She had been telling him
of the country vicarage where her early years were
spent under the care of her father, "the dear ole
vicar—the ole home, dearie—I can see it now—
with roses all around the door and Gawd is Love
over the mantelpiece in fretwork—and a governess
cart and a pony in the stable—and rabbit-shooting
at Easter and prayers every morning—I can see it
now, dearie. I was a fine gel then—the old dad
was that proud of me—I got engaged to a viss-
count. Well, one day, dearie, a stranger come to
the Vicarage, and the ole dad in the kindness of
his heart gave him shelter and—— *Oh, can't-
someone-kill-those-bloody-birds-I-can't-'ear-meself-
think!*"

Greenstockings stood up. " 'Ere, stop it, Florrie.
Come on 'ome, dear. You're prop'ly blotto to-
night."

"Blotto be damned! Shan't! Don' wanner
g'ome. And don' in'rup' me when I'm talkin' to
frien'. You go'n' make those bloody birds shurrup.
They're doing it a-purpose to 'noy me."

"No, they ain't, dearie. You come on 'ome."

"Shan't! Not till them birds shurrup. You go'n' stop 'em. Else I will."

"Now, Florrie dear!"

The birds danced about their cage, screaming, cheep-cheeping, and chirruping to the merry bang of the beer-engine. With a surprisingly adroit movement the drunken Florrie stretched a huge arm, grabbed her pot of beer, and flung it fiercely upwards at the cage. It did its duty; it drenched the birds, and their debate ended abruptly in a flutter of wings.

Greenstockings turned wrathfully upon her friend.

"Oh, Florrie, you *cruel* thing! Oh, Florrie!"

Florrie got up. "I'll learn the bahstuds to in'errup' me."

She put a foot on a chair and reached up to them.

"Le'm alone!" squalled Greenstockings in impotent anger. "Oh, the pore li'l things! Le'm alone, Florrie. Oh, you beast!"

Florrie held in her hand a lighted match. Greenstockings flew at her and grabbed her about the waist. Florrie shook her off, and the trouble began. She came down awkwardly from the chair and swerved towards the kid.

"Eh? Whassat? You call me a beast? I don' 'low no-no-body call me a beast. Who er you to call me beast—eh? You—yer mangy skinnygalee

—you—yer little rag-tag street baggage what I
could pick up and put in me pocket—you!"

The drink was in her brain and in her eyes. She
was big and strong, and she knew it, and, being
drunk, was ready to demonstrate it. She saw
before her a little slender body, taut with anger,
but consciously shrinking at its own daring. She
shot an arm across the table behind which it shrank,
and grabbed it by the throat.

"Come out—you! Beast, am I? I'll learn yeh!"

Bang! went the table to a running comment of
smashing glass. In the next minute horrid things
happened. The big girl and the little girl fought in
naked fury. Florrie aimed blow after blow with
the fist at the little, worn face, while Greenstockings
responded with the teeth, and bit at the hand that
held her, and kicked and screamed. As the teeth
met, Florrie howled and dropped her hold. Greenstockings flew in then, and clawed at her, ripping
from her neck the cotton blouse, and tearing with
frantic fingers at her breasts. She butted with her
head, and used her feet with dire purpose. Both
sobbed and emitted animal noises.

Then Florrie forced her to the lounge, and got
her down, and gave back what she had received,
and more. She tore her blouse from her, and
clawed and thumped her, pulling her up and beating
her heavily down, and tearing at her bare arms.
Together, in a frenzied embrace, they rolled from

the lounge to the floor. Greenstockings drummed with her feet, and struggled and cried under the torture of Florrie's hands, and bit again and again. Then Florrie found her throat and closed upon it, and her eyes glared down upon her victim. She was not then choking Greenstockings, her little comrade. She had her hands upon an enemy, upon the embodiment of all the unkind things that had befallen her; and she was wrenching its life from it. No cries came from Greenstockings now; only hard moans that grew fainter and fainter.

In less than a minute had all this happened: before any of the customers could follow its action, and before the landlord had had time to come round from his private room behind the jug-and-bottle bar.

Then two of the Malays leapt from their corner and fell upon Florrie. They leapt just in time. Scarcely a breath was left in the torn body of Greenstockings. But Florrie would not be denied her vengeance. She freed one hand and strove to beat them off; but they were two to one, and they dragged her back from her enemy. But they could not hold her. With lithe movements she fought them, and broke from them, and, ere Greenstockings could stir from her prostration, seized her again.

"And this time I'll finish yeh, blast yeh!"

Again the Malays came to her, and she fought them and Greenstockings by turn. Manfully and

whitely they stuck it. In a few moments they had
bleeding faces and torn clothes, and many times had
rolled in the muck of the floor. But at last one collared her low, beneath the breasts; and the other
seized an arm and twisted it. In this way, only,
could they save the poor thing that Florrie hated.
Straining, panting, their black faces smeared, their
mouths open and steaming, they dragged her from
her friend. Writhing within their arms, she
screamed, blasphemed, and spat. But slowly they
staggered with her to the door, and paid no heed to
the curses she laid upon Greenstockings and the
tale of horrid punishments that she would inflict
upon her when she got her alone.

Then, as they pulled back the swing doors with
their feet, Greenstockings sat up, and looked about
her. She looked round for Florrie, wondering from
which corner the next blow would fall, and could
not see her. When she did see her she saw her
struggling in the arms of two agile black men. Next
moment Flash Florrie was free. A piercing cry
shocked the attention of her captors from their
charge, and an antic figure leapt upon them and
overwhelmed them with worse words than Florrie's
and with sharper fingers. A bruised, bleeding, tattered little figure was upon them, shielding Florrie
from them with outstretched arms, and crying:

"Grrr, yeh dirty blasted niggers! Leave 'er be!
'Ow dare yeh put yer dirty black 'ands on a white
gel! Leave my pal alone, yeh bloody niggers!"

TWELVE GOLDEN CURLS

XV

TWELVE GOLDEN CURLS

THE little home of Quong Lee in Limehouse
Causeway rang with the noise of the evening
revellers of the Quarter, for a feast was in celebra-
tion. Across the blind of his window, lit by the
shop lamps of the narrow street, raced and raced
the antic shadows of those who danced and frolicked.
But Quong Lee is old and wise, and sits apart from
youth-time pleasures. As I entered his room, I
entered purpurical darkness in which the window-
blind made a single slab of radiance. In a corner
about half-a-yard from the floor glowed a bead of
blue light. The air was loaded with the reek of
chandu. The light spoke swiftly and softly. "Ao.
Baitho!" it chanted. I stood by the door and wondered how I could be expected to find a seat in a
room which was blank with darkness and bare of
furniture. Then a match spluttered, and Quong
Lee shuffled to his feet, lit an oil lamp, put his pipe
away, and showed me a cushion on the floor.

He bade me welcome; asked if I had eaten my
rice, and could I lend him half-a-dollar? I could

and would, on condition that he told me an entirely new and true story. He accepted my condition and my half-dollar; and, while the crowding noise of the festival rose to alcoholic pitch, he spoke somewhat in this wise:

About these great docks of London, not a while ago, lived one Nobby the Nark, who lounged about the water-side, and ran messages for men; or, more accurately, proceeded at a moderate pace upon such occasional business as other men might require of him. During the day, when not thus occupied, he would meet men who took sums of money from him, and promised him six to four, or, it may be, ten to one, should the results of certain performances by horses, which were to take place in the afternoon, be favourable to their doing so. At evenings he would frequent the gaming-rooms kept by the honourable Ho Foo. Sometimes he would gain a little, and sometimes he would lose much, for very highly skilled was Ho Foo in games of hazard.

There came a night when Nobby the Nark would play pinkipo and chausa-bazee, games that do not lightly yield their benefits to the cumbrous mental processes of those who do occasional work at the water-side. Very seriously did Nobby strive with the games, but at the night's end honourable Ho Foo held not only the cash of Nobby, but the scrawled promise of Nobby to pay very much more.

Now it was imperative that Nobby should hasten to redeem that promise; for, should he fail to do so, he would be for ever forbidden the gaming-room of Ho Foo, and Ho Foo would pass the word to all other gaming-rooms; and life without a gaming-room would have but little savour for Nobby the Nark.

Four days passed into the upper air, and no word came to Hoo Foo from Nobby of the money that should fulfil the written promise. Now Nobby was the father of a daughter, who kept house for him, and worked for both of them at an adjacent factory; and this story to which the honourable mister deigns to listen is properly the story of this daughter.

On the evening following, Ho Foo was taking the air around the gates of the West India Dock, where the seamen gather to talk, when he heard soft sounds as of one ill at ease. Drawing near he saw, in a dim corner, this daughter of Nobby. He knew her well; for often she had come to his gaming-room to drag her father home. Very fair was this maiden, and brave was her carriage. Upon her head were many honey-coloured curls, cunningly held captive by a little time-worn hat; and her bright voice never failed to please those to whom she addressed herself. But to-night her carriage was subdued, the curls had escaped, and some hung pendulous; and about her large eyes hovered many tears. Now to the keeper of a gaming-house nothing is more moving than the sight of distress; and Ho Foo approached her and engaged her in sympathetic talk.

As he heard her tale, sorrow and anger rushed upon him, and he reproached himself that his gaming-house should have brought such disorder of mind upon so fair a maid. For, from her words, he learnt that Nobby, her father, had encountered much difficulty in procuring the necessary sum that should redeem his written leaves and admit him once more to the gaming-tables; and, growing fretful from this continued abstinence from his favourite pastimes had bade her go out to the dock gates, where gathered the seamen, and procure it by some means from them; nor should she return to their home until she had done so.

Emotions of an unpleasant nature enveloped the mind of honourable Ho Foo at this, and he folded his hands and turned his thought, inward. Thereafter he spoke, saying:

"This one is indeed in torment at words of daughter of Nobby the Nark. O maiden, go home, go freely home. Turn from this base resort and go home in tranquillity. Return to altogether despicable one, Nobby, and say to him that his written leaves are restored to him. Take them, little chrysanthemum, and put your mind in order, and fill your heart once again with emotions of agreeable nature."

From the fold of his canvas jacket he produced the written leaves of Nobby and presented them to her. These words were not the true words of honourable Ho Foo, for he spoke in something of his fathers' tongue and something of that of this country; but his attitude of mind conveyed itself to the maid; and there sprang into her face that which told him his words were good to her. So they parted; she happily, to her father, no longer fearful of what the night might bring; while Ho Foo passed on to take the air, and his mind walked in the clear spaces of right-doing.

But there were certain base men, hirelings of the law-givers, who, knowing nothing of this right-doing, fixed their eyes upon his wrong-doing in disregard of their laws against gambling. And so it fell one night that a company of men set out from an office of the law, and entered the gaming-house of Ho Foo, and haled him before the justices. There they laid two charges upon him: that he was the keeper of a gaming-house, and that he had in his possession many ounces of the Great Tobacco. Heavy was the sum that he was commanded to surrender to them ere he might go free; nay, all he possessed, and more, so that he was driven to sell the things of his house that he might satisfy them.

Much wisdom was in the mind of the sage who observed that the misfortunes of one are the entertainment of the many. Ho Foo was now driven to sleeping in a poor back room, empty of any appointments; and there he lay unheeded, while about the streets his downfall occasioned much agreeable diversion among his friends and those who had frequented his tables.

There he lay, and to his uneasiness of mind came sickness of the body. None came to succour or to nourish him. On the bare floor he lay in misery; and those who heard of his plight said that they hoped others were providing him with what was necessary. But in a space of days, the tale of his sickness came to the ears of the daughter of Nobby the Nark; and her heart was moved and she was sorely troubled. She had not forgotten—what woman would?—his beautiful service to her in her distress, and she cast eagerly about her for means to help him. But alas! turn as she would, she found none. Ho Foo, she had been told, was stricken with a fever, and his malady demanded fresh fruits and cool jellies and gentle draughts, which were not to be had for the few pence that remained from her week's wages after household dues were met. She even looked about their miserable attic home lest there might be something that she could spare on which some shillings might be obtained. But nothing was there save the poorest and most necessary appointments of daily life.

Then, one morning, as she dressed hastily for the factory, pondering still the case of Ho Foo, and looking blankly into a chipped scrap of mirror, it suddenly came to her that she had long been carrying money about her person. It was in her hands now, fine coils of spun gold which she was piling loosely upon her head. There lay her means of succouring Ho Foo, and the aid would be sweeter and more potent since it was part of herself.

Well, that evening, when she came home from the factory, she sat down before the scratched mirror, and let down her hair, which tumbled in a cascade of light. Slowly, sadly, yet glad for the service that she might bring a friend, she took scissors and cut off a curl from either side, and laid them on the table before her, and wept upon them. Then, resolutely, she cut two more curls. So did she yet four times more, till twelve golden curls lay spent upon the table. These she made into a small parcel. Then, 'barbed and cropped of her beauty, ludicrous to look upon, she crept out to one who had dealings in hair. And when that one saw the refined quality of the hair, his eyes glistened, and he turned his mind into itself for a space of minutes. When he spoke he named a sum of money which, he said, he might with great ado recover when he should have treated the curls with the skill that was his; a sum utterly inadequate to the purpose for which it was required. But the large experience which the maid's penury had given her in bargaining came to her aid, and much talk and manœuvre passed between them, until at last she left with many shillings.

Then did she hasten to procure delicacies and comforts for poor Ho Foo; and O my son, this child, shorn and disfigured as she was, careful as she was of her fair name, steadfast as she was in bearing herself properly before her neighbours, hesitated not to go to the bare room where lay my countryman, and tend him, and lave his head, and feed him with the dainty foods that he was too weak to give himself. Bold was her spirit in thus challenging the good report of her kind and imperilling her bright fame; bold her spirit and very tender her heart. Many nights she went to him, and gave him of her care, and sorely grieved was he when his eyes discovered the sacrifice of her beauty. He would have refused her ministrations and her baskets of delicacies, but she would not hear him, and he was indeed too weak to contest. So she continued to visit him till the store of shillings was spent. Then she came no more. But her work was done, and soon Ho Foo was able to rise and take the air of Pennyfields.

She came to him no more. Many days he lingered about West India Dock Road, hoping to see her, and tell her of his thankful heart. He would not go to her, lest he thus bring base remarks upon her; he would wait at corners, thinking that she might pass. But she came no more; and at last he dispatched a little boy as messenger to say that he again was well and was burning prayer-papers in her name for gratitude.

Ill-tidings came back with the messenger. Her sweet service had driven the fever from Ho Foo, and it had entered into her. On the bed in her attic she lay, broken of beauty, and suffering, while her ill-famed father gave her what casual attention he could spare from the water-side and the gaming-room.

Meekly did Ho Foo plead to Nobby the Nark that he might be permitted to attend her; to sit at her door in case of urgent need; to perform domestic duties. But Nobby the Nark replied with coarse words and evil insinuations and brutal looks and snarls. So Ho Foo could but wait in the street outside, and watch, and call his good spirits to her aid.

In a few days it was done. From that poor attic she passed, even as Ho Foo stood in the street below, with bowed head, as he had stood every day since his first visit.

But that is not the end. When the news came to him, Ho Foo went from that darkened street with a high resolve. A few small coins he had;

and when he had performed rites above them, he took them to a gaming-house, then newly opened, and his good spirits went with him. He came away, long past the noon of night, and his belt was weighted with many coins and rolls of paper money.

Next day he sought piously for the merchant in hair; and when he had found him he inquired of him concerning twelve golden curls recently bought. And lo! there, in a small box, they lay, even as they had been delivered. Then did Ho Foo inquire the price at which the merchant would relinquish them; and when the merchant demanded of him four times that which he had paid for them, Ho Foo quietly counted out the money and carried the curls reverently to his room.

Sorrow and misfortune had come at once to two poor people remote in birth and creed—Ho Foo and the daughter of Nobby the Nark—and from this bond sprang love everlasting. For, with the rest of the large sum of money that he had won, Ho Foo opened a little tea-house in the Causeway; and in a corner of that tea-house he made a shrine; and in that shrine he hung the twelve golden curls, and beneath them he wrote fairly, in his own characters and in the characters of this country, their story; and the place is known as the Tea House of the Twelve Golden Curls.

The Tea House of the Twelve Golden Curls is built on sacrifice and gratitude; and there, because of one white girl's gracious heart, your countrymen and mine now gather in friendship and pass the hours in amity. And if any dispute ever arise between a white man and one of us, it is the custom that if one of them cry, "Let us talk of it at the Tea House of the Twelve Golden Curls," the dispute is ended, and courtesies pass in place of angry words.

And that is the story of the Twelve Golden Curls.

"Quong Lee," I cried indignantly, "it isn't true. I don't believe a word of it. The Chinese and the whites don't dwell together in amity. You know as well as I do that they don't. And there's no tea-house here called the Tea House of the Twelve Golden Curls."

But Quong Lee was impenitent. Placidly he picked up his hap-heem pipe. "The words of the elegant visitor to this despicable hovel," he remarked, "have much truth. The nature of the relations at present existing in this quarter between the white men and my countrymen is undoubtedly not to be described as amicable. Even to-day, if the nobler sort of Englishman observes a Chinaman gaze upon a white girl his instincts of chivalry are aroused, and he indites stern epistles to the Printed Leaves. Which is precisely the reason why this one has just invented and related the unprofitable and wholly fabulous story to which the refined and exalted mister has so politely listened."

MISS PLUM-BLOSSOM

.

XVI

MISS PLUM-BLOSSOM

IT is the tale of the wooing and winning of Lily Lily-Ling, called Miss Plum-Blossom; of how she was pursued; and of her capture by her neighbour and countryman Sam San Phung.

Miss Plum-Blossom was London-Chinese, and first saw the fog of this world on a cargo-boat as it crawled up the Thames from the great seas. She was registered as a native of Stepney, but her round face and blunt features and olive skin furnished a clear *dementi* of that statement. For eighteen years she had lived among her countrymen, seeing little of the other corners of London which are not Chinese, and now was under the care of Lee Tack, known as the Dragon-with-Jaws-of-Fearful-Proportions, which is to say that he was a bad man; and she worked as serving-maid at his establishment.

Now Sam San Phung, as he took tea and bitter melon at the tea-house of Lee Tack, cast slanting eyes upon the melting beauty of Plum-Blossom, and would have prepared for her a shrine in his two-roomed cottage in Gill Street. But lo! there arose another, one Ah Toy, the Mighty One of Bodily Perfection, who had much fame as a vaudeville wrestler; and upon Miss Plum-Blossom he cast direct, disconcerting eyes, so that he dazzled her.

Where to bestow her heart the maid knew not. She had walked in Poplar Gardens with each, and with each had given and received certain salutations. But somehow . . . Ah Toy was strong and clever and admired, and he had money; but he came from Canton. Phung was poor and shiftless, and cut but little ice; but he was of Mongolia, like herself, and, like herself, was registered as a native of Stepney. Greatly she desired to escape from the uncouth voice and hands of Lee Tack; but when she decided, in her mind, for the one, her heart turned straight to the other. When she was with Phung she wanted Ah Toy; when with Ah Toy it was Phung who seemed desirable. So it is with the young maid throughout the world.

And so the merry comedy went on; and when the two men met in the Limehouse streets or about the West India Dock, Ah Toy would thrust forth the mighty stomach that had made him famous, and beetle upon his withering opponent. And when he had passed Phung would turn and make the sign of spitting and the five fingers.

But the happiness of Miss Plum-Blossom was at length achieved, and this was the way of it.

It was the night of the Feast of Lanterns, in mid-

January, and Limehouse was doing its utmost to let
London know about it. In Lee Tack's tea-house
carnival reigned, and Miss Plum-Blossom was trot-
ting backwards and forwards with tea and cakes
and noodle and chop suey and illicit drinks. From
a table beyond the farthest depths of the tea-house
came a volume of noise that beat against the noise
of the streets, and those near the doorway, who
sat in the line of the two waves of sound, were
drowned beneath them. ⊺⁻ the back room, before
a table, stood Sam San Phung, and with him were
Lee Tack and Ah Toy. Ay Toy was making his
presence known.

"Ho Ess! Dissa one he say to hon'ble Sam San
Phung 'at he fight with dissa one, and if dissa one
he t'row hon'ble Sam he tek Miss Plum-Blossom."
He swayed slightly, for his bulky form was the
more bulky by many doses of rice-spirit. "And if
hon'ble Sam he t'row dissa one, 'en he tek Miss
Plum-Blossom. For Miss Plum-Blossom she no can
say wedda she like dissa one or hon'ble Sam, so dissa
one he――"

But here Lee Tack stepped forward with the
dignity of a mandarin, and raised a fat yellow hand.

"Dissa one he wan no fight in dissa mis'ble litty-
o-saloon. Ho no! Hon'ble Ah Toy he wan fight
cos he heap big fighting fella. Ho, Plum-Blossom!"

Plum-Blossom trotted forward at the call, and
sidled to the table, her hands playing at her throat

as she glanced from one to the other. Her flat face showed perplexity.

"Which you like for husband?" demanded Lee Tack. "Hon'ble and upright Sam San Phung or noble and round-bodied Ah Toy?"

"No can say," she murmured after a pause, scanning Lee Tack's face as though fearing she should do wrong whatever answer she gave.

"Ho!" snapped Ah Toy, "if the son of a seaslug, Sam San Phung, no fight——"

Again Lee Tack silenced him.

"Fighting no good," he declared. "No equal chance. You t'row cards, huh? Dissa one bring five card, and plenty number he win—huh?"

Miss Plum-Blossom, still immobile, nodded. Ah Toy grunted. Sam San Phung looked agreement. Lee Tack clapped and gave an order for cards. While they waited, Sam San Phung moved to the girl, and took her hand, and prattled a moment, until Ah Toy thrust out his stomach, and sent Phung staggering back many paces. Lee Tack raised a reproving arm. Then from between the curtains that concealed the staircase swam a figure carrying a pack of Chinese cards.

The news had galloped round the tables in the outer room and had been passed to the street; and soon the room was full. The musicians ceased playing. The boys stopped dicing. Two pipe-smokers alone remained placid. The rest of the room

centred, in a tangle of oily heads, about the little
wicker table in the centre. Lee Tack took the cards,
cut them, and dealt five to each man. Ah Toy took
his five and looked at them; and curses dropped
from his lips like spitting toads. Phung threw first
—defiantly, a two. There was a bubble of exclama-
tion as Ah Toy threw four.

Ah Toy delivered an unnerving grimace, and the
men pressed hard on the players. Phung turned a
little pale as he threw three, and Ah Toy followed
it with two. He raised an arm, and pleaded with
the crowd:

"Back, Foo; back, Sway Lim."

Plum-Blossom watched with impassive face, wondering whither the cards would send her—to the
bold Ah Toy or to the gracious Phung.

"Move! Move!" pleaded Phung again, as the
crowd hung heavily around him. He moved a hand
to his head, and pressed them with his elbow. He
threw eight. Ah Toy swore, and cleared the audience with a jerk of the arm as he threw eight,
followed by nine from Phung. But they crowded
still closer now, watching for the last throw. It
was not the excitement of the prize that held them.
A woman—what did it matter? But the result of
a gamble—that did interest them.

Ah Toy wiped his nose on his arm and threw,
airily, a six. They stood now Phung twenty-two
and Ah Toy twenty. What would the final cards

do? The next throw settled it. Phung, with a wooden face, wiped his brow, stretched his neck, and turned up his last card—ten.

There was a noise of indrawn breaths. The great wrestler was beaten, and the girl was Phung's. Ah Toy broke back, lifted up arm and voice, and declared his intention of inflicting upon Phung a chastisement that would cause the utmost discomfort and degradation to him and his totally insignificant ancestors; but Lee Tack, alert for forms and ceremonies, caught his arm and recalled him to a sense of the proprieties. He opened the door. From the street came crude music and the shuffle of feet. Then the curtain was twitched aside, and the giant form of Ah Toy was propelled into the midst of the street revellers.

Well, Plum-Blossom was Phung's, and he paid the bridal money and took her home with him. And next day the wedding feast was held at Lee Tack's—a feast of many dishes, with wines, whisky, rice-spirit and fruits. When the barbarity was at its height of heat and clang, Phung slipped a hand to Plum-Blossom and they shuffled from the restaurant, and out to Gill Street, and so to the shrine that he had prepared for her, radiant with blue and silver and ivory, and odorous with punk-sticks.

But on the fourth day after the card-drawing there were those who twitted Ah Toy. They twitted him with the loss of Plum-Blossom, and they twitted

him for not showing better form when wrestling
the previous night on the stage of the Poplar Hippo-
drome. And they twitted him for being outdone
by a poor thing like Sam San Phung. Whereupon,
being a little discommoded by the existing order of
things in this and other worlds, he went from café
to café and from pub. to pub., and drank much
ongaway; and at the Blue Lantern he finished with
gin, and called upon his ancestors to assist him in
wreaking vengeance upon one who had wrought
such removal of gravity among those who had once
respected him. He swayed from the bar, and
marched with conquering, if erratic step down the
by-way of West India Dock Road to Gill Street, to
interview this Sam San Phung. He flung his tre-
mendous weight upon the door, which was not
fastened, and so precipitated himself into the front
room of his enemy. A friendly table helped him
to recover his dignity, and he looked around. At
first the room seemed empty; then he saw Plum-
Blossom alone, and an enormous smile spilt his
moon-like face. As she was now the property of
Sam San Phung, she would serve his purpose of
vengeance equally well.

Behold him, then, lurching upon her. Behold
him mouthing to her in explanation of his unhappi-
ness. Behold the gin taking command of him, and
impelling him to weep tears of self-pity. Behold
her shrinking from him, with little low exclamations

of terror. Behold him grasping her in his rolling
arms, using her with the rage of the man who is
softly answered.

But now—a quick whisper of feet on the stairs,
and a sharp cry behind the combatants. Ah Toy's
hands fell. He turned. Behold the insignificant
son of a water-rat, now transformed into an outraged husband, fearful in dignity. Behold Sam San
Phung in the doorway, face peering, mouth screwed.

He howled and sprang into the room. He slid
to Plum-Blossom, grasped her, and drew her against
him. Instinctively Ah Toy bent low, arms outstretched. Phung saw the movement, and understood. This Ah Toy would fight him in his wrestling
way in which he was an acknowledged master. Well,
Phung would fight in his own way, and avenge the
disgrace of the mauling of his Plum-Blossom. For
some moments the men stared at each other: Ah
Toy, truculent, hands and face working, Phung immobile. Plum-Blossom shrank into a corner, her
little robe of blue linen drawn about her slender
limbs.

Ah Toy took a preliminary step, playing for an
immediate throw from which the water-rat would
arise crippled. Phung did not meet the challenge,
but fell back till he stood by the little cupboard in
the corner. His right hand disappeared. Mr.
Jamrach, the St. George's dealer in wild live-stock,
does not get all the live-stock that is landed in Lon-

don. Otherwise Phung would not be as happy as he is to-day.

Suddenly his right hand reappeared under his tunic. It quarrelled nervously with something. Then it shot forward, and something went full at the face of Ah Toy. At the sudden touch of the furry, quivering thing he fell. The thing crawled about and fastened itself now here, now there. He delivered a high-pitched and far-reaching cry, and fought it with his hands. Then he grabbed it. It fought him hideously, with tiny claws and teeth, and the champion wrestler screamed. Hero on the mat as he was, this new opponent had found him out. He rolled, and fought to find his feet while fighting the thing; but, move as he would, the thing was about him at all points.

At last, with a spasmodic heave, he scrambled to his knees, and drew his knife. The monkey's teeth were in his arm. He slashed at it, and missed, and blubbered, while Phung stood away and smiled and smiled. The second cut got home. The monkey fell; and he dashed for the door. Phung, still smiling, shot a lightning foot. Ah Toy fell again, and again the little claws were about him; but this time he was up swiftly, dashed it away, and with a twist brought the great knife down to Phung's left side. There was a rip of cloth. Phung fell. Lurching and blubbering, Ah Toy bolted through the door.

And now Plum-Blossom awoke, and gave a cry, and would have fainted. But Phung was up and at her side at once. He gathered her in his arms, as one would a flower, and soothed her with gentle phrases. Her little hands ran all about him, fearing for her lord's safety. The knife—where did it go? He was wounded, yes—he was in pain?

But no. Oh no! He opened his tunic, showing the long slit made by Ah Toy's knife. He displayed the blue shirt, which showed no mark at all; for inside the tunic, which he threw open, hung something that had been sliced through, and had saved him.

"Phung's mascots, O Springtime Blossom of the Plum Tree. Mascots—all-same devil-chasers— give Phung his Plum-Blossom for bride, and save Phung's life."

With quick fingers he detached them from the fastening that held them, and showed them to the wondering Plum-Blossom. Then, with salutations, he placed them before the little joss in the corner. There were two Chinese cards, such as could be slipped from the tunic while pressing the crowd back in a hot room; the nine and ten which, produced at the right moment, had won for him the game in Lee Tack's saloon.

He picked up the gibbering monkey and stowed it in its basket beneath the cupboard. He stretched hands to Plum-Blossom, who trotted to him. He laughed.

"Ho!" Ah Toy come here no more. Phung make him plenty frighten. Ho! embrace me, *paopei*, embrace me—nine and ten times!"

THE CANE

— XVII —

THE CANE

THE schoolmaster of the mixed school in the
dock-side quarter was a most circumspect
man. He walked, as it were, in a frigid and dry
odour of sanctity. He took himself and his position seriously, and his manner was fitting to his
calling. He looked upon himself as the keeper
of a charge. The young, rude citizens of the future
were under his care, and it behoved him to walk
warily and so comport himself as to bring no faint
suggestion of the indecorous before the notice of
the young minds among whom he spent his days.

Living in this fashion, he was, to a large extent,
severed from the realities of life, and there were
many subjects and aspects of subjects upon which
the young minds could have enlightened him. But,
by his training and calling, he was incapable of
crediting children with personality. Children were
children, and youth was youth—or, as he preferred
to name it, young life. The child was not, to him,
a soul, but an immature adult. His class was not
a class of boys and girls, but grouped specimens of

Child. As a giraffe was a giraffe, so a child was
a child. Such-and-such would a child think upon a
given subject; such-and-such would be its conduct.
He had got the child-mind standardised and taped;
and that was all there was to it. Psychology in the
schoolroom he dismissed. He had passed his exams.,
and was a school teacher, and possessed all the
qualifications which, according to his managers,
completed a teacher's equipment. These managers
did not include imagination as part of this equipment.

School and lodgings and a seaside holiday in the
summer were his life. Theatres were beyond his
means, and few new books were obtainable. His
evenings he spent in his bed-sitting-room, correcting
exercises, rereading his old books, or discussing the
newspaper with his landlady, and smoking two pipes
of tobacco. A walk round the houses preceded bed.
He chose his walks carefully: there were such terrible places in the neighbourhood—public-houses
and low places of entertainment. He gave these
places a sad glance and walked hurriedly past them,
lest he should receive contamination which might
affect his pupils. Apart from their reputation and
unsavoury atmosphere, he never would have entered
these places. So conscientious was he, this meagre,
parched little man, that he felt that he must, like
the clergy, hold himself aloof from all human
pleasure save of the mildest sort. He must stand

outside even the suggestion of reproach; and he had therefore enforced upon himself total abstinence from liquor. He strove to be a shining example and, like King Wenceslas, to exude moral worth and integrity from his very footsteps.

His school was a mixed school, and he took classes of girls and boys alternately. The scholars were gathered from the two-roomed cottages of the side-alleys of the district, and were a difficult team. The street was their first playground, and when they came to school the task of breaking them in to concentrated study was no casual matter. Born in those cramped alleys, and running wild from babyhood, their sense of social values was choked in birth. Among the methods of breaking them in, the managers gave first place to corporal punishment, administered indiscriminately to boys and girls alike. They held that it was the only punishment the children understood, and that it showed beneficial results; and inattentive or unruly girls received the cane from the men teachers in the same measure as the boys.

When he had first taken up his duties he was much averse from observing this rule against the girls. He was a shy man, and the mere fact of taking a girl's class had somewhat perplexed and disconcerted him. The order to inflict punishment with the cane when, in his opinion, the children merited it, still further abashed him; he had even

protested. Somehow . . . it seemed to him . . .
it wasn't quite . . . But the managers said "Rub-
bish," and pointed out that this was a low and unruly
district, and that they were a rough lot of girls
from slummy homes, and he would have endless
trouble and disorder unless he followed the school
system. It was all for their good, and he would
be failing in his duty as teacher if he did not use
these measures. If they were not taught to behave
now, they would never learn: they would follow
their elders of the district and develop into street
wastrels. They concluded by telling him not to be
silly, and there was then nothing more to be said.
When, at any time, he was told not to be silly, he
collapsed, for he recognised that worldly wisdom
was not his strong point; and if a thing were accepted as usual, he, too, accepted it without further
examination.

So, in a few weeks, he had become accustomed
to the school and his classes, and now inflicted
punishment on the girls, perfunctorily and in an
absent way, whenever their conduct required it,
and thought no more about it. He had discovered
the truth of what the managers had said about
unruly characters. Naturally nervous, he hated disorder of any kind, and soon found that without
the cane he could not maintain quiet.

He thought no more about it for some years.
Then some silly busybody, without knowledge of

the district, discovered the practice of this form of discipline, and wrote to a leading daily paper about it. Quickly it became public; and, when other newspapers took it up, in a large way, the story of this school where girls were caned by men, a storm broke over the school and its managers. Letters appeared denouncing the "odious practice," the "frightfulness" of it, the "appalling degradation" of it, for masters and pupils. For weeks the controversy raged, and drastic action was threatened; but a sudden political crisis arising at this point, the papers dropped it, and it passed out of the public mind. The managers ordered that the system should continue.

The public controversy led, naturally, to discussions among the teachers, who dismissed it professionally, as a journalistic "stunt;" as foolish vapourings by people who didn't understand; and it led this particular teacher to a study of the correspondence. This correspondence set him thinking. Some of the arguments advanced against the practice were curiously vague, full of dark hints that were strange to him.

He began to be disturbed. He began to take an interest in the matter, and to find in these letters much that he had never before perceived. Grim, covert suggestions had been made, and they remained with him. He remembered having read somewhere that every man carried with him a demon,

and he had accepted the theory—about other men.
Had anyone suggested that he nursed a demon, he
would have laughed. But that week something
happened that filled him with fear. He had occasion to call out for punishment a girl who had
hitherto given him no trouble; Dolly Latham, a big
girl of thirteen. Dolly was pert; dark of hair and
eye and gay-footed; a girl of apple-blossom, pink
and white, adumbrating the golden beauty to come.
She moved with the delicious insouciance of the
child, mixed with the first conscious grace of woman;
and the shy, uncertain lines of her figure carried in
their promise as much beauty as the perfect achieve-
ment.

The thing that startled him, that left him sitting
scared and dumb at his desk, was, that after he
had used the cane upon her, and she was returning
to her seat, she flashed a backward glance at him
from the depths of her big eyes: a glance that
linked itself in his mind with the curious things
upon which he had lately pondered. Until this
day he had hardly noticed her. She had given little
trouble, and had been to him but one of a group
of children, a unit, identified only by a name. It
was not until this close relationship occurred between delinquent and master, and that curious
glance. . . . It sat upon his mind.

Next day he had occasion again to punish her,
and a sharp emotion swept over him and drove out

the detached judicial motive. An emotion which filled him, on the one side, with disgust, as he tried to ignore it, and, on the other side, with a cold and dark delight. He feared it and fought it while secretly hugging it. That night he walked home in a mixed state of concern and abandon; and his landlady noted his condition, and he was conscious of her attention, and cunningly gave her cause to think he had been drinking. This low subterfuge, so unusual to him, set him wondering still further about himself. He hardly dared to think, lest he should discover somewhere in a recess of his mind something that knew and understood the cause of his disorder.

He wanted to talk to his colleagues about it; to discover whether they, too, had suffered these queer disturbances on similar occasions; but he felt some awkwardness in approaching the question. If he introduced it and threw out hints, they might mark him as a monster. Perhaps he was a monster. Or perhaps it was stupid sensitiveness on his side. From the attitude they had taken on the newspaper attacks, it was clear that they were in no way troubled by their duty and thought nothing of the detailed indictments. It was a part of the day's routine to which they gave no consideration. No, he could not talk to them: he could only wonder and speculate, and, by wondering, he slowly fed this strange disorder.

All through the class hours he was conscious of the girl, and began to notice that, from this raw, unkempt herd, she stood out bold, bright, alert. He found himself making a mark of her, and doing deliberately what hitherto he had done perfunctorily. He seized every trivial occasion to indulge himself with this intoxicating power, concentrating upon her, and even manufacturing excuses for calling her out; and when her large eyes clashed with his he was filled with a quiet ferocity. He wanted to hurt her. He flicked and lashed her with his tongue throughout the day, holding her up to the laughter of the class; and he noted, with a pleasure he could not stifle, the slow crimson that crept up her face as the chosen words stung her. He dared not honestly recognise the dreadful enjoyment that was his as he stood over her, cane in hand, and she stood shrinking before him; and how each gasp of pain that he drew from her was coldly echoed within him. But something in him did recognise with horror that Dolly set herself in every way, by inattention and unruly behaviour, to challenge him. The more often she was whipped, the more she seemed to presume some sinister alliance between them; unspoken, yet known to both.

"Can't think what's come over my genterman lately," his landlady said to her next-door lady. " 'E don't seem like the same man. Always was

quiet, but 'e's got quieter lately. And a funny way
about him—sheepish, like."

He grew more and more morose, shutting himself away from all intercourse. He began to wonder whether the ideas that rambled in his mind
were perceived by others. It seemed at times, to
his heated fancy, that the girls of his class began
to give him closer attention. Each time he punished a girl it seemed to him that they watched
him with cute, secret glances. When he called
Dolly out, she walked out flirtatiously, and it seemed
to him that his class was one broad grin. He knew
that all of them were aware of the newspaper
attacks on the school, and he began to wonder if
they saw; if they knew. But it was of Dolly that
he most thought. No matter how severe the punishment, always, as she returned to her seat, she would
toss that backward glance of understanding. He
began to want earnestly to talk with her; to discover
what that bright head held; to reassure himself that
she was just an idle, careless hoyden of the slums,
answering discipline with the facetious defiance of
ill-breeding.

So he thought and thought, and day by day the
beast grew within him, and night by night he would
go home to his lodgings, stricken. Horror walked
at his elbow and plucked at his sleeve, and stabbed
him with wink and leer. He lived in a spate of light
intoxication, as though a fluent fire were playing

within him. He began to cast about him for means of escape from this possession. He thought of re-signing his position, and finding another school where the custom was not in operation, but the thought of change was startling to him: he had lived in this district for twenty years now. And some quiet, chuckling voice inside him said No; a quiet voice, but stronger than the strongest of the op-posing voices.

He knew now what it was that he nursed within him, and he ceased to think or to care. He sur-rendered himself to the exquisite drug, and thought with delight of the secret paradise to which he had access.

And one afternoon, when he had dismissed the class, he kept Dolly in, and punished her in private, ferociously, and talked with her.

It was late when he let her go, and the sidelong rays of the evening sun as they slid through the schoolroom windows slanted upon his desk, and a poor, crumpled man that sat before it, bowed and sick. When, after some long time, he raised his eyes they fell upon the school cane. With a sudden effort he roused himself. He sprang from the chair, seized the frightful thing, twisted it into many shape-less fragments, and hurled it to a corner, with horrid curses upon those who had compelled him to use it.

Then he took his hat and coat and went out. He was last seen on a wharf at the river's edge.

THE SONG OF HO LING

THE SONG OF HO LING

BEHIND the small candle-lit windows of a cottage in Poplar High Street maladroit fingers were plucking from a Chinese guitar a yearning song of two notes, and a metallic voice was singing out of time and out of tune with the guitar. Fingers and voice belonged to young Ho Ling, and the song was a song of Acknowledgment and Avowal. On the first notes of the song the curtains of the window opposite were twitched aside, and between them appeared the head and shoulders of Amber Goldstein. About the head and shoulders swirled an eddy of dense auburn curls, and the bright mouth and fine nose were lit by yet brighter eyes. A girl of spirit and ability.

Nightly this ceremony was performed. Nightly at six o'clock Ho Ling would drag his guitar from its place beneath the bed and carry it to the window; and there he would sit and sing to Amber Goldstein his song of a service rendered and of an holy obligation as yet unfulfilled, but to be fulfilled at whatsoever time he should be called upon

by his benefactress, the young lady across the road.
And nightly the young lady would appear at her
window and smile a quick acknowledgment of his
declaration of fidelity. And Ho Ling would smile
back, worshipping the marvellous, pale, bright
beauty of her.

Very pious was Ho Ling in his observance of
the teachings of the Four Books. None so devote
in worship of his ancestors and in service to his
aged father with whom he lived. None so careful
a student of the Book of Filial Piety and the I-li
and the Li-Chi. From the hands of the white
woman across the road he had received a service.
He was under a deep obligation to her. His faith
required that that obligation be discharged; now
or later, he or some other member of the house
of Ho must serve that woman at any time when
she stood in need of service. Nothing must come
between him and the performance of that solemn
duty. He must wait and watch until occasion arose
for the redemption of his assurance.

The favour which she had bestowed upon him
was of a somewhat intimate nature; nothing less
than misleading the police in their marshalling of
evidence against his old and too gay-hearted father.
It was Amber Goldstein who, for some womanly
whimsy—possibly some amused concern at the impotent despair of Ho Ling; possibly some fleeting
thought of his forlorn butterfly smile—it was she

who smeared her fresh lips with a lie, and proved
to the police that old Ho Wong was not a bird,
and could not be in two places at once. Dearer
than life to Ho Ling was this aged and roguish
father of his. For him he lived and worked and
strove, and sometimes stole, following the precepts
of the Books; and a service done to the old man
was esteemed by him more highly than a greater
service done to himself.

The charge was that old Ho Wong was concerned in the stabbing of Lop-ear Langford, an
officer of the Blue Lantern's Army of Hiccupation.
The charge was truly laid. Lop-ear Langford had
pulled the nose of Ho Wong and had knocked over
his drink: "learning the yeller bahstuds to keep their
places," he called it; and the night following Ho
Wong had waited in an alley-way for the Lop-ear,
and had used his knife upon him in a way sufficient
to justify a conviction for causing grievous bodily
harm. Two people saw and identified Ho Wong,
and the case looked bad for him. In exceeding
agitation of mind and body, his dutiful son went
about the Quarter, seeking to discover some who
had seen his sire at that hour in other places; but
as he had but four or five shillings to his hand, he
found none who could say, assuredly, that they had
seen him.

It chanced, however, that the two witnesses
against him had themselves made frequent appear-

ances in the dock, and the magistrate hinted to the
police that such witnesses required corroboration.
This could not be brought; wherefore, when Amber
Goldstein voluntarily came forward, and stated that
Ho Wong had spent the whole evening in her shop,
playing chess, the charge was dismissed. For Amber
was a respectable young woman, with a thriving
second-hand clothes business. The police had no
official knowledge of her, and agreed that her testi-
mony might be considered as unimpeachable.

Upon this, young Ho Ling came to Amber with
many protestations of gratitude, desiring to know
in what manner he might repay her. But Amber
made light of it; dismissed it, airily, as a matter of
no consequence; as a thing that was done perfunctorily, the outcome of a mood, carrying with it
nothing to justify a second thought. She did not
say that virtue was its own reward; but she implied
that she had done this to please herself, and that
there was nothing to make a song about. But
Ho Ling ransacked his poor room; and came across
with gifts; a cast-off opium pipe of bamboo, a Chinese banner, two little tasselled devil-chasers, an
empty ginger-jar and his guitar. But Amber would
have nothing. She smiled upon his gifts, and
refused them; and when he pressed them upon her,
she drove him, in mock exasperation, from her shop,
and commanded him never to mention it again.

But he was not so easily quieted. What was

to her a trifle, an idle digression, an unrehearsed gesture, was to him a sacrament, a precious gift, something whose value could not be weighed or measured or computed; something that would rest upon him and his family until requited. Had it been a mere casual service, costing her nothing, its effect upon him would have been the same. But it was more: she had made a sacrifice for him; she had told a lie in his behalf. It could not be forgotten.

And, deliberately flouting her statement, that it was nothing to make a song about, he retired to his room and made a song about it; and, as I have told you, sang it to her every evening thereafter.

His honourable papa, however, was not so zealous as himself in observing the precepts of the founder of the ancient line of Ho, and the song made frequent quarrels between them. Ho Wong's attitude towards these matters was rather that of the white man than the yellow—"I didn't ask her to do it. If it pleases people to go out of their way to help others, let them do it. If they didn't like doing it they wouldn't do it. We didn't ask for it. We have given thanks, and that's enough." And he rated his son soundly for wasting his evenings by singing to Amber Goldstein, and hanging about her shop during the day, watching for opportunity to serve her. And as young Ho Ling loved his father, he suffered under these reproaches.

Often he tried to make his father acknowledge the solemn obligation under which the house of Ho rested, but his father only made signs with his fingers and spoke the Chinese equivalent of "Rats!" It seems that his father had little respect for the ancient house of Ho: so long as he could eat his rice in tranquillity he felt that he could comfortably leave the house of Ho to look after itself. Veneration of family history, usually strong in fathers and weak in sons, was here to be found only in the son.

Ho Wong spoke further, and in harsh terms, of his son's subjection to this white woman, fearing that she was doing him a bit of "no-good," and was making him neglectful of his true business of touting for lodgers for the lodging-houses—on commission —and thereby reducing the slender income and supplies of rice-spirit of himself. It did not need a peevish father to observe that Ho Ling, from gratitude for service rendered, was speedily drifting towards a deeper feeling for the benefactress.

"She is a woman, and she is white, O son with the brains of the peacock. If she looks thus fondly upon you at evenings in response to your song— which, to my untutored ear, is as the grinding of iron wheels upon sandstone—it is because she desires to ensnare you and work her guile upon you. This person, who has seen the passing of many years, might—were he to cast off the restraint of experience—find something not wholly displeasing in her

pale-faced beauty. But I am past your age, and
am wise—and poor. Think not that I speak against
her out of rivalry with you. Were I dowered with
your youth and vigour and attainments—*and
ignorance*—and she smiled upon me, I do not say
that I would not in some measure imitate the accomplished manœuvres of the duck expiring under a
thunder-storm. But it is not so. I am of an age to
be read in the ways of woman. Mysterious and
deadly are they all towards men, and most dark
and hostile when they are white-skinned. Therefore, O son, take heed. For there is that in the face
of the white woman which is not for your good.
She will bring sorrow upon you, my son. Ay, and
sorrow upon me also. Did you not last week bring
home a barely-to-be-looked-upon three shillings for
the sustenance of your much-enduring father? Take
heed."

Whereto Ho Ling lifted up his voice and cried:
"O my father, nothing holds with me before the
desire to serve my august and venerable father.
But is it not clear to you that but for this white
woman my august father would be languishing in
a cold and indescribably dreadful English prison,
eating the food of coolies and toiling for white masters? O my father, great debt our house owes to
this woman, for she saved us from dishonour and
you from misery. I cannot look upon her without
thinking of that load of service to be discharged.

Surely virtue and beauty must dwell in one who could so venture herself as to render service to us who are nothing to her?"

To which old Ho Wong again spoke the Chinese phrase implying "Rats!"

But a week later the occasion of their quarrel was removed. Opportunity was given to Ho Ling to redeem his vows, and set free the house of Ho from its obligation. He came home on Saturday evening, and handed two shillings to his venerable father, as his week's allowance for social dalliance; and when his father demanded more, he replied that his labours had been but ill rewarded that week, and there was no more, save what should keep them in food. And his father rose and employed terms of no-veneration against his son, accusing him of having wasted time upon the white woman which might better have been used in earning money. He spoke of himself as suffering under emotions of the most disagreeable and hardly-to-be-endured nature, and went angrily.

Left alone, Ho Ling moved for awhile about the room; then, having sung his evening song, and waited vainly for acknowledgment from the opposite window, he too went out and mixed himself in the melancholy turmoil of Chinatown's evening. He walked up West India Dock Road, and stopped at the Causeway, and stood looking along its narrow length. In its primrose twilight many figures

strolled, stood, shuffled and turned. He stood in
blank indecision for some moments; then, moved by
some impulse, he glided into its inviting dusk, and
passed through it to Narrow Street. Along this he
walked some way until he came to the derelict
wharves. Here he stood for some moments snuffing
like a dog at the dark perfume of the water-side,
and gazing across the river, which threw up a leaden
light.

He was turning to the Causeway again when he
heard voices. He looked round, and saw nobody;
but from behind a pile of rotting barrels fell a
cascade of sibilants; and following it a firm, sharp
voice: "You leave me alone! D'y'ear? Else I'll
call the police!"

The voice of Amber Goldstein. Hot upon it followed the thin, shrilly voice of his father, who spoke
English so chaotically that even sailors could not
understand him. Ho Ling moved forward to get
a view of the disputants and discover what was to-do.
Here were his two nearest ones quarrelling: he must
intervene, and skilfully, without giving offence to
either. As he turned the corner, Amber's voice rose
again. "I dunno wod yer talking about. But you
leave me alone, yeh dirty beast! Else I'll——"
And he saw that his father held Amber by the wrist,
and was pushing her, and that she stood on the edge
of the wharf with her back to the water. A moment's loss of balance and she would be over.

Without thinking, he sprang forward to place himself between them and part them. But, as he did so Amber, already scared, saw only an antic figure leaping upon her out of the dusk; and, anticipating some fresh peril, tried to step aside to avoid it. Flurried, she missed her footing and slipped. She slithered and kicked for a moment over the edge of the wharf, and grabbed the sleeve of Ho Wong, who had her wrist. Then, together, they shot over into the river.

A flood-tide was beating up; and Ho Ling saw his father and his benefactress struggling against the currents. Neither, he knew, could swim. A quick glance satisfied him that there was no boat within hail and that the wharf was bare of rope or belt. He knew that he must go in; he knew that with that tide running he could not save both. In that moment, he was faced with a frightful problem. Which must come first—his sacred blood-tie with his father or the equally sacred obligation to the white woman who had served his house.

Through his mind flashed the words of The Book of Filial Piety enjoining utmost sacrifice for the parent's sake; and with them the words of Mencius on the solemnity of discharging services rendered by strangers. His father was at the point of death, and he could save him. But his benefactress was in like position, and he recalled his song and its solemn vow made before the joss. Here now was

the opportunity to perform that vow and discharge
the obligation from the house of Ho. Now or
never—for he knew that Amber Goldstein had no
family, no blood-relation upon whom he might later
discharge it. Now was the time or for ever he
must wander with this burden upon him and his
house, this unrequited service to lie as a curse upon
his children and their children's children.

Yet his father—dare he neglect him even for such
a vow as this? After all, his father was a man,
a father of a son, and this other was but a woman
—a white woman. Too, she herself had made
nothing of the service, and had persistently declared
that it called for no reward. But there were his
vow and his song. Yet the most holy of all ties
bound him to his father. What would be said of
him by the spirits when it became known that he
left his father to die and saved some white woman?
Yet how would he stand when the charge was made
that he had left a benefactress to die, with his ob-
ligations undischarged, when the power to save her
was in his hands? There was the unchangeable law
of requital of service and sacrifice; the more stringent
in such a case as his, where the service was bestowed
by a white. And there was the everlasting law of
utmost duty to parents.

For two seconds Ho Ling stood, while he thought
of these things. This short, sharp conflict of instincts, battling with each other, lasted no longer.

Then, his head whirling with the combating impulses, he dropped his canvas coat, poised on his toes, and leapt to the water. As his head split the water, the icy shock of it cleared him, and he made his decision. With sturdy strokes he swam towards one of the struggling figures.

Which?

THE END